For Marion

Steven's Vocation

with gratitude for
your long term help
and support.

Joe Bakewell

11/20/01

Steven's Vocation

Joseph J. Bakewell

To order additional copies of this book, contact:
Xlibris Corporation
1-888-7-XLIBRIS
www.Xlibris.com
Orders@Xlibris.com

Contents

To my number one fan—my protective and loving wife.

CHAPTER ONE

Sunday afternoons were always sad, especially that last hour of freedom before supper at six and study hall at seven. It was the hour when boarding students who'd been home for the weekend checked back in, and I, having stayed on campus, felt most lonely. On one memorable Sunday in early December of my freshman year, I sat in my room thinking about Christmas vacation while I waited for someone to talk to. I didn't realize, until much later, that during that Christmas vacation I would see the first signs of what would become the greatest tragedy of my life.

There was a sound in the hall; I got up and looked out to see Frank Cooper opening his door.

"Doyle, did you hear the news?" he asked.

"What news?" I strolled toward him and followed him into his room.

He dropped his bag on his bed and turned around. "The Japs have attacked Pearl Harbor."

I shrugged. "So? Where's that?"

"Man! You should buy yourself a radio. It's in Hawaii."

I sat on his bed. "*Hawaii?*"

"Turn on the radio," he said, as he took off his coat and hung it on the back of his door. I moved over to his desk and turned the knob on his radio. I started to diddle with the tuner and volume.

"It has to warm up," he said, and he came over to take charge. "All the stations have it," he said. He tuned in a strong station and went back to unpacking his bags.

I sat listening to what little was known at the time. "My God," I kept repeating.

"See, I told you," he said.

Out in the hallway, things were livening up as more boarders checked back in. Everyone seemed to have a different twist on what was happening; there were a few who, like myself, hadn't heard about it until just then. Fagan had heard the news on his dad's car radio just before being dropped off. "My dad says that the Japs are probably on their way to California right now," he said. That got a real argument going.

Stan Kawolski, a senior and a football player, announced, "I'll join the Marines right after graduation. We'll see how the Japs do when they can't sneak up on us." Others joined in the fervor, stating what service they would join, and why. Jenkins, my roommate and a sophomore, said, as an aside to me, "Just think, Doyle, you're a Church student. You won't have to go at all." I was about to argue when Kawolski said, "Forget it, kid. The war's gonna be over in a couple of years." The conversations continued as we all headed down to the dining room for supper.

Normally, our routine was: supper at six, study hall from seven to nine, and lights-out at nine-thirty. Seniors got to stay up until ten. That night, before saying 'Grace' and a prayer for our servicemen, Our Headmaster, Father Harris, announced that we would all go to the chapel at seven o'clock. Suddenly, I wished that I could go home. I wanted to be in a *real* place, a place where I knew the people, the adults, and could rely on their opinions. If my father was sober, his opinions were usually thoughtful, and he had all kinds of smart friends whose opinions he quoted. This war thing was certainly exciting, but it was starting to sound scary.

There were only forty-eight boarding students at Seton Hall Prep; the rest of the student body of 550 boys consisted of 'day hops.' Boarding students lived on the third floor of the 'Prep' building, along with several teachers who served as proctors. Father Harris also had rooms on our floor. We lined up in the hallway that night and marched to chapel as a group. There we were joined by the junior seminarians from Seton Hall College, which shared the campus.

Monsignor Morris, who was president of the college, presided at the service. It was nothing special, having been arranged on such short notice, just a few hymns and a decade of the Rosary. Morris spoke briefly about the need for extra prayers and sacrifices in order to insure the victory, which would surely come. Twenty minutes later, we were back in our building getting ready for study hall.

I don't think much studying got done that night, by me or anyone else. I sat there in a daze trying to make some sense of what had taken place in the last two hours. Why, at such a dramatic moment in history, did I feel like I'd been relegated to the sidelines? Jenkins was right; I was a Church student and wouldn't be expected to defend our country. I'd be like the women and children, protected by the real men. How had it happened? I couldn't remember doing anything, but I must have; everyone knew that I was going to be a priest.

"So, you think you're gonna be a priest, heh?" It was my Aunt Kate, one of my father's sisters. She was all Irish and loved to give people the 'needle.' I could never tell if I was being set up for something, or if she was being sincere—a rare event. We were at a birthday party for my cousin, Pat. It was at Aunt Mable's house in Astoria, where my grandmother lived, as did all of my father's sisters and their families. My father was the only boy and the youngest sibling. In answer to her question, I just shrugged.

"Hmmn," she said, "your sermons are gonna be something—very popular."

"Excuse me," I said, getting up to feign interest in a game being organized by my cousins, anything to escape. How did she know about the priest business, anyway? I hadn't made up my mind. All I did was agree to go to the Catholic grammar school in the next town for my eighth, and last year of grammar school. It was probably all over the family, but at least my mother's sisters wouldn't make a big thing out of it. It wasn't hard to figure out how Kate knew; my father needed something to brag about to his family.

I hated those Doyle family gatherings. My cousins were all older than I, and were all very talented, according to their mothers. They got to sing, recite and dance. Nobody wanted to see what I could do with a penknife or a yo-yo. They were also brilliant, so bringing my report card wouldn't have helped.

The part I hated the most was the first few minutes after we arrived from New Jersey having traveled at least an hour by bus and subway. My father would bring me in to say 'hello' to Grandma. The ceremony never varied; she'd be sitting alone in the front room looking out the window. My father would push me to a position directly in front of her. "Say hello to Grandma." I did as I was told.

"What's that? I can't hear him," she'd say to my father.

"Say it again, Steven."

"HELLO Grandma."

She'd nod at me over her glasses. "What's that he's got on his ear?" she'd say to my father.

He would bend over, carefully examining my ear, my shoe, or whatever else she picked on that Sunday. "It's a bit o' dirt he picked up on the subway."

"Well, you can wash it off, can't you?"

The rest of the day was better, even if I was completely bored. Later, somebody, not my father, would give me a nickel for an ice cream. Toward the end of the day, I got nervous in anticipation of the ride home with my father, who invariably was half in the bag.

The bell rang announcing the end of study hall; we were all back in the hallway. Somebody called out, "They sunk our biggest battleship. The President's on the radio." We all scurried to listen.

The war was all we talked about for the next two weeks. The news was universally bad, but nobody wanted to mention the possibility of our losing, or of our being invaded. We all felt that we had to tell the other guys about relatives, mostly uncles, who were in the service or reserve units. I had one

lace. One of my little sisters had left a toy on the kitchen floor and she'd slipped, hitting her head on the stove.

People at home, including my parents, seemed to be just as confused by the war as I was. All except my uncle, Bert, that is. He worked at CBS News in New York. He knew all the correspondents and helped prepare the broadcasts. He and my aunt, Eileen, lived in Fort Lee, the next town, I could easily walk there.

"Don't you worry, Steve, things may look bad for a while, but once we get going they'll wish they'd never started this thing," Bert said.

He gave me some maps with all kinds of arrows and other markings on them showing how it would probably go. I felt that I was in possession of some kind of secret war plans. I couldn't wait to put them up in my room back at Seton Hall. My parents were not as interested in my maps as I expected. I think they felt that Bert was a bit of a blow-hard, overly enamored of his position at CBS where, as I later learned, he operated a teletype machine.

Anyway, at least my uncles hadn't gone off to fight yet, and my father said that it would be a long war, which we would probably win.

That Christmas vacation was significant because of the war, but what sticks in my mind even more is the way in which it cemented my feet on the path toward becoming a priest. It had all started innocently enough; three years earlier, I wanted to be an altar boy. Every Catholic kid wanted to be an altar boy. You had status, you got to go on the altar, into the sacristy, to hold the plate under peoples chins when they received Holy Communion. At High Mass, you got to sit next to the priest and look out over the congregation, knowing that many of them, with nothing else to do, were looking at you. You also got to walk through town with a clean white surplice over your shoulder, and even to make some tips at weddings and funerals.

At first, I fumbled around watching the other kids for

directions on what to do, all the while dreading the day when I'd have to perform on my own. My day came soon enough when the older kid didn't show up. My dread proved well founded. I rang the bell at the wrong times, and had to be told several times what to do by Father Paxton, in a stage whisper heard throughout the church. At least I didn't need to be told twice, and I showed up. Soon I was serving more than my share of the Masses.

One morning, I think it must have been in December or January, because it was still dark when I arrived to serve the seven-thirty, I found myself kneeling on the first step of the altar, noticing that the candles were fading in and out and moving away and back toward me. Father Paxton, a large imposing Irishman, was droning away in Latin until I heard him say, "The wine and water," in his stage-whisper voice. I remember whispering back, "Yes Father," just before slumping over onto the higher steps in front of me.

I lay there for several minutes before he turned and told me to go into the sacristy. I was so scared that enough blood got to my head for me to get up and move off the altar.

There was a bench in that little room, just off the altar. I sat there and removed my surplice and cassock for what I thought would be the last time. Father Paxton finished the Mass, went into the priest's sacristy to remove his vestments and then came to deal with me.

"Get up and come with me," he said.

I followed at a respectful distance, out the back door, across the walkway, and into the rectory next door.

He took me into the kitchen. "Here, drink that," he said, handing me a tumbler.

I took a drink. It was wine and tasted awful.

"Drink it down," he said.

I drank it, thinking that the cure was worse than the disease. I had to sit down.

He gave an order to Margaret, his little old Irish housekeeper, "Give the lad some breakfast, some eggs and bacon."

Oh, God, now she was going to be mad at me, the source of more work. He went into the dining room to wait for his own breakfast. Margaret went about her business with no expression of any kind. She looked my way. "I can just go," I whispered. She shook her head, looking a little bit cross. I sat and took in my surroundings. In every direction, things were tidy and cleaner than in any house that I'd ever been in. The floors were shined and spotless; there was the slight smell of cleaning solutions mixed in with that of bacon being fried. Woodwork was everywhere, framing the doors and windows and along the hall and in the dining room. It all shined.

She had Paxton's breakfast on a tray. Before carrying it in, she put a cup of tea and a piece of toast in front of me. The tea was delicious and the toast was gone before she came back. She smiled.

I got my breakfast in bits and pieces: another piece of toast, some jam, eggs, bacon and more tea. Each time, she'd bend over and say something, softly in my ear, "There, you were a bit hungry now, weren't you? You look Irish, are you Irish?"

With my mouth full, I answered mostly with nods of my head. She seemed strangely happy.

That was the day when my journey started. I served Mass almost every day, and Paxton would say, "Come over and have your breakfast." I don't know how he knew, or even *if* he knew how much better those breakfasts were than the hot milk on bread, or the occasional bowl of Wheaties, that I got at home. Margaret always smiled when I came in. I'd sit at my place in the kitchen, already set, and have my breakfast while Margaret softly spoke to me of her past life, especially her days as a pretty colleen in Ireland, and threw in bits of gossip about 'Himself,' as she referred to Father Paxton.

My involvement grew; I found myself doing all kinds of yard work around the rectory and church. My reward was a dime, and sometimes a quarter, from Paxton, and great lunches and snacks from Margaret. Often, she'd send me home with a little something: a piece of cake, a couple of cookies, an occasional holy picture. She'd put it in my hands and then grasp my hands between her own and say, "God bless you."

I think in some ways, Paxton enjoyed seeing her spoil me, even if he did needle her about it sometimes. He never said much. If he knew anything about me, he must have gotten it from Margaret. I was surprised when towards the end of my seventh grade school year, he told me to have my father come and see him after Mass that Sunday.

My father rarely went to Mass; I had to tell him what the Gospel was on the days we went to see his mother, so that he could pass muster with a lie. I'd catch hell if I forgot, or worse, got it wrong. He went to Mass that Sunday, and I walked to the rectory office with him. Margaret let us in and we waited in the office until Paxton made an entrance. He sat behind the desk, looking like some kind of high government official, and announced to my father, "I believe the lad has a vocation. You should get him out of that public school and put him in the Catholic school where he belongs. I'll see to the rest of his education."

I can't remember my father saying anything, but he fairly beamed. He looked as if he'd won the lottery. On the way home, he talked to me more than he had in the last six months. At one point he said, "That's one thing they'll have to respect, a priest in the family."

It went easily from there. I was transferred to the local Catholic school in Fort Lee for my eighth and final year of grammar school. The nuns and other kids treated me a little bit special at first, but after a month, the boys forgot about my special calling. I was always a good student and used to being a teacher's pet so my treatment by the nuns was nothing new. It was the girls that bothered me. They'd been with the same boys for seven years; I was a novelty for that reason alone. They also seemed to be intrigued by the whole priest business. I got lots of teasing, and I was ashamed at how much I enjoyed it.

Toward the end of the year, one of the girls had a party, and I was invited. I knew all the boys from the games we played during recess and occasionally hanging out after school, but the girls were separated during recess, and after school, I usually went right home to Coytesville, where none of them lived. The nuns were ever present during school hours, and a future priest would not want to be seen talking to the girls. Part of me dreaded that party, but another part flew off on wild fantasies.

I had never kissed a girl. I hoped that there would be some organized kissing games so that I could appear to be just being a good sport while finding out if it was as wonderful as I imagined. I rarely talked to the girls, but I certainly noticed, was entranced by, their breasts. I had no idea what they felt like.

The party disappointed. The boys hung out together, there were no kissing games, although a few of the bolder boys took girls outside or to another room. Their reported exploits made me burn with envy. Arlene took me outside, but we just talked; I didn't know if she wanted me to do something, or not.

That summer I worked for a landscape gardener, and, on my own, mowed a few lawns, including the church's. I rode my bike to Fort Lee once to visit Arlene; she wasn't home. Starting prep school was a great relief to my boredom.

CHAPTER TWO

That first Christmas vacation from Seton Hall also required another agonizing visit to Astoria and all the Doyles. That visit put another brick in the wall enclosing me in the role of future priest.

It started in the usual way. I was ushered into the front room to say 'hello' to Grandma. She looked at me, just as she always did, over her glasses, but this time she surprised me and spoke directly to me.

"Do you have enough clothes?"

"Yes, Grandma."

A critical examination of my clothing followed. "Are you able to keep warm?"

I nodded, "Yes."

She gestured with her hand, "Come over here."

I closed the three or four feet that separated us, and went to the side of her rocking chair, the one with all the padding, and the well-worn spot on the wooden arm, where she rested her hand while saying her rosary.

She took my hand and looked up at me. She pressed an envelope into my hand and said, "Buy yourself some clothes, something warm, and pray for me."

I hesitated. If it had been my Nana (my mother's mother),

I would kiss her. So, I did. For the first time, I kissed my grandma, something I had always wanted to do. I bent down and kissed her forehead.

She nodded and then fluttered a hand at me. "G'wan now."

It was the Irish way, but I saw her blinking her eyes as I left, and she went back to looking out the window.

Aunt Kate was more like her usual self. "What do the other boys think of your wardrobe?" she asked.

I don't know how she knew that my clothes were such a sore spot. I had only a few things that fit; the rest was a collection of hand-me-downs. Maybe it was my overcoat. My father got it from a hock shop, and it looked like something Basil Rathborne wore in a Sherlock Holmes movie. It had a ring around the cuffs from wear by its previous owner before my mother let the sleeves down.

"They're not all rich," I said. I had heard from my mother that Kate had needled my father about the rich kids at prep school giving me the cold shoulder.

"You could use a few things though?"

I shrugged and nodded, "I guess."

"This should help," she said, handing me an envelope.

By the end of the afternoon, I had five envelopes.

As soon as we left to go home, my father asked, "How much did you get?"

"I don't know."

"You don't *know*? Let me see; give me the envelopes."

I handed them over, a little sick inside. I didn't like taking money. I wanted to think of the envelopes as gifts. I especially didn't want my father to have this money, to take it and drink it up as he always did if I didn't hide my money in a safe place.

"Wow! You did all right, forty bucks." He gave me back the envelopes, and that was the end of it.

I still hid the money when I got home.

The rest of the vacation went as I expected; I served at Masses and let Margaret chew my ear off about how Paxton was keeping her a virtual prisoner while he spent a lot of his time palling around with the police chief in Fort Lee. I knew Chief Connors, he lived on my street in Coytesville. He had twin daughters, both as plain as white bread. He seemed like a nice guy to me.

Father Paxton took me for a ride one day. We went to Jersey City and visited his friend Monsignor Bailey, the pastor at Saint Anne's, a very large and wealthy parish. Bailey turned me over to a curate; who showed me around. The church was big and impressive, but it didn't take very long to see it all. Father Desmond, the curate, took me back to the rectory where he treated me to a Coke and some pie. We sat in the priest's dining room; Monsignor Bailey had his own, more formal dining room. Desmond asked me questions about myself.

I looked around; after all the glory of the church with its gold leaf and stained-glass windows, I thought that the priest's quarters would be luxurious. The room in which we sat had a door at each end and a long table down the middle. The table was covered with white oilcloth, and one wall had a counter along its length with cupboards above it. All the finishes were just plain wood, or were painted white. A crucifix and some holy pictures hung on the other wall.

"How did you know when you had a vocation?" he asked.

"Oh, I don't know; it just sort of came along."

He grinned. "God didn't knock you off a horse, like he did with Saint Paul?"

I laughed, "Maybe that's why I'm afraid of horses."

He tipped his tea cup while holding it against the table and looked into it. "That's okay, Steven, hardly anybody can answer that question."

I nodded, feeling a little more comfortable.

"How do you feel about girls?" he asked.

My stomach clutched. "I don't know much about them."

He leaned back in his chair, looking me over, as if assessing my answer. "Well," he said, "all you need to know is to stay the hell away from them."

"How do you do that after you're a priest?" I asked. This being a question I'd been pondering for some time.

He sat up and laughed; it sounded a little forced. "You'll have a lot of people watching you."

I wasn't sure how that answered my question, but he got up, indicating that we should move on.

On New Year's Day I served Mass and on the way home thought about my resolutions. At the top of the list, being the only item so far, was getting an 'A' in Latin. I walked down that steep hill behind the church on that dreary morning wondering if my old man would still be home sleeping it off by the time I got there. I thought about going a block out of my way, over to the main street, where I'd meet some people and say, "Happy New Year." But I decided to keep trudging along and work on my resolutions. I needed one having to do with becoming a priest. That was it. I resolved to stop just going along with it. I would look at the bright side and find good things about being a priest. Yes, what a great idea! It might even help me to stop thinking about girls, about breasts, and from having those tormenting fantasies.

A few days later, while I was packing to go back to school, I noticed that one of my mother's eyes seemed to be getting worse, more swollen. She said it had gotten infected, and that she'd get something for it.

At school, I was surprised to find out that the war had displaced girls as the main topic of conversation. I knew it wouldn't last, but it did make it easier to keep to my new resolution for the priesthood. Everyone had come back with new opinions and information on the status and direction of the war, and I enjoyed some minor notoriety with my Uncle Bert's war maps.

American eyes were fixed on the South Pacific and what was happening in the Philippines. Opinions were all over the lot:

"My father says that MacArthur will suck the Japs into a trap and wipe them out."

"Yeah? My dad says that MacArthur is a pompous ass. He should be court-marshaled for letting the Japs take him by surprise. He lost his whole airforce, they were caught on the ground!"

I tried in vain to get a word in and tell the guys what *my* father had said. It was on New Year's Eve; he was drinking at home, for a change. Or, he was at least continuing to drink at home, having arrived at home slightly stewed and carrying a good supply of beer. We were in the kitchen, and we listened to the news while he drank and smoked. At the end, he switched the radio off and turned to my mother. "It's the goddamned English. They've got Roosevelt wrapped around their finger. We're not sending stuff to MacArthur; it's all going to Churchill."

My mother was not overly interested in politics, but she knew what she didn't like, and she did not like the English. I never knew whether that was because of what they did to the Irish, or because her English father had abandoned her family when she was a child.

"What will the Irish do?" she asked.

"They're just staying out of it, from what I can see," he said.

"They should help the Germans," she said.

This was too much for me. "But, Mom, we're at war with the Germans."

She turned to look at me with one of those half-smiles, which said that someday I'd find out how these things *really* work, and then she turned back to the sink.

In less than a week, girls regained the conversational lead with sports and the war tied for second. As I prepared to go home for Easter, Bataan fell, and Corregidor looked like it was on its last legs. I had an uneasy feeling when I heard people talk about how we were still going to win.

I had been doing a little better in maintaining a positive attitude towards becoming a priest. My Latin was a little bit better, a C+, but keeping my mind off girls was tough. I went to the chapel every day after track practice and asked God to keep my mind pure for the rest of the day. I also took the advice that a priest had given us, and shined my shoes whenever thoughts came to me while I was alone in my room. It was supposed to absorb your mind in something else.

Jenkins came in a couple of times when I was busy with my one pair of shoes. On one occasion he said, "Where do you think you're at, Doyle, West Point?"

"I just feel better when they're nice and shiny," I said.

I went home for Easter with one objective: to line up a job for the summer. My mother suggested that I try the Columbia Presbyterian Medical Center at 168th Street in Manhattan. It was just a short bus ride across the George Washington Bridge, and the bus terminal was right across the street from the medical center. The next day I went up to the highway and got the number 86 Public Service bus to go and apply for my first real job. When I told them that I'd been a patient there, and admired everyone on the staff, I got the job. I didn't tell them what I thought about waiting for hours on long wooden benches with the other charity patients in the clinic, or how I fought off going to the bathroom for fear of missing my turn.

Because of my youth, I had to get New York State working papers. That meant a visit to a state doctor downtown. All I remember of that was standing there naked, and the doctor saying, "You should try and get more to eat, and watch your posture. A tall kid like you has to learn to stand up straight."

I said, "Yes sir," and left vowing to stand up straight, and wondering how I could possibly eat more than I already consumed at every meal.

I stopped in at the rectory on my way home.

Margaret was delighted to see me. "You look starved. Can you have a piece of cake?"

"I've given up sweets for Lent."

"A sandwich then, and a glass of milk."

Between bites of my sandwich, I told Margaret about my new job.

Father Paxton came walking through in his shirt sleeves; he needed a glass of water. He barely acknowledged my presence before announcing, "You'll be serving the High Mass on Sunday. And then tomorrow after the seven-thirty you can help Helen with the candles on the altar."

That was it; I'd be serving Mass every day on my vacation. "Yes, Father."

He turned and started back toward the hall. "She's not as tall as you are; she needs help."

I shrugged at Margaret. She smiled and came over to pinch my cheek. "It's so good to have you here."

It was getting late by the time I got home. My mother was pleased that her job idea had worked out, and we worked together to fix supper and get the girls into bed. After supper, she wanted to play cards. We played two hands of rummy, and then she set her cards down and started to talk. I studied her face; she looked good, no sign of her injuries. She told me of her first job; her older sister had gotten her a job at the phone company. With her first check, she had treated herself to a lunch at Schrafft's.

We were sitting at the table in our little kitchen. The table, with its worn and peeling red-and-white checkered oilcloth covering, sat alongside the refrigerator, just across from the green-and-yellow gas stove with the dried drippings around the oven door.

"I wish that I could get out to work again," she said. "You're lucky."

"You will. Maybe Aunt Eileen could take care of the kids."

She shook her head. "Eileen has her own troubles."

"It wouldn't be so bad if Pop stopped drinking, would it?"

She sighed, "I don't get out at all."

She was changing the subject. It was getting dark; I got up to pull the bead chain on the overhead light, which didn't help much because of the stupid frosted shade around it.

"I just get out a few times a week to shop. By the time I get the girls ready and get to the stores and back, the day is gone."

I sat and listened, trying here and there to say something encouraging. She'd acknowledge my statement and then go on. It was getting late; I was tired after my big day.

"His mother would always give him money for drink, you know. She wanted him to fit in."

The light was playing tricks with my eyes. I began to not hear her words, instead I watched as my mother faded off into the distance, getting very small and then coming back to life size. At some point, I must have started to slip off the chair.

"Steven. Steven. It's getting late."

CHAPTER THREE

Helen was a member of the Rosary Society and the principal caretaker for the altar. I had seen her many times, usually at a distance when I was on my way out after Mass. She always wore dark colors and clothes that seemed too large, along with frumpy hats, which fit close to her head and down close to her ears. I don't think I ever saw her hair, or at least, not much of it. She was twenty, or maybe a little older, and had a sweet face. I always thought that she'd probably become a nun someday, so I never thought about her like I did most other girls.

After Mass the next morning, I put away my cassock and went back out on the altar to help Helen. There's a feeling that comes from putting out the candles and leaving the altar at the end of Mass, and then entering the same area moments later when the church is empty, and the main lighting is turned off. It's a feeling of intimacy, a more spiritual feeling than when the church is in use.

I found Helen busy trying to scrape some candle drippings off the altar cloth. The drippings hadn't come from my work; only amateurs let that happen when they were putting out the candles.

"I'm so glad that you're going to help me," she said, "I have difficulty moving the tall candles."

She smiled and I looked at her, close up for the first time. She wore only a touch of lipstick, and her skin was clear and very smooth. Her dark eyes shined in the subdued light. She was actually pretty, and the more I looked, the prettier she got. I noticed that her baggy clothes didn't hide everything.

We worked together; I held things up and she cleaned under them; I handed things down and put them back. She said that I could leave after all the lifting was done, but I stayed to help with the dust-mopping and tidying up.

At the end she went down in front of the altar and motioned for me to come and admire our handiwork. I went and stood next to her. And then it happened: she put her arm around my back and her hand on my shoulder. She pulled me close and grinned, "Isn't it nice?"

I turned to her and whispered, "Yes," unable to comprehend how I could be standing in front of God's altar with a hard-on.

She turned to go. "Are you coming?"

I had to think of something. "I forgot something. I'll be right back." I almost ran back to the altar boy's sacristy and got a surplice to carry in front of me.

She was waiting outside the front door. "I just wanted to wish you a Happy Easter," she said. "Does the Easter Bunny come to your house?"

"Sure, I hide the eggs for my little sisters."

We were on the sidewalk. "I hope the Bunny brings something just for you," she said, and she turned to go.

I headed in the other direction and sat down on the wall behind the church. I looked at the surplice on my lap. I wondered if she even knew what a hard-on was?

On another day, Father Paxton took me with him to visit a woman whose son had gone down with his ship in the North Atlantic. He'd joined the Merchant Marine before the war. He was on his third voyage when a German submarine torpedoed his ship. I learned that a body could only last for two minutes in the cold waters of the North Atlantic, and that no other ship in the convoy could stop to pick you up for fear of being torpedoed.

I wasn't sure what to expect, or what I was supposed to do during the visit. I guessed that Paxton just wanted me to see how priests handle these matters. Mrs. Graham was glad to see Paxton, and very cordial. She virtually ignored me, and I didn't know how to react. Was I supposed to do something? Say something? I sat off to the side and didn't move, or say anything.

When we were at the door, getting ready to leave, I said, "I'll pray for your son."

With her lips tightly closed, she nodded, more in my direction, than at me.

Back in the car, Paxton started the engine. "He was her only child. Women should have more than one."

He shocked me; it seemed such a heartless thing to say. I nodded, but said nothing. By the time we got to the rectory, I was thinking that there was at least a certain logic to what he said, but it still wasn't right.

Bataan fell; the Japs had a plane called the Zero that sounded unbeatable; Rommel was beating the ears off the Brits in North Africa. The only good thing that happened was the Doolittle raid on Tokyo, and people were saying that it had been mostly for propaganda.

As summer vacation came on, I thought less about the war and more about my new job. I thought of it as my first opportunity to get out into the real world, to experience, first-hand, what adults were always talking about.

I escaped from Seton Hall with a C-minus in Latin and headed for the hills of Coytesville. One of my first stops was at the rectory; I wanted to convince Father Paxton that I would only be able to serve Mass on weekends. He accepted this without argument, but gave me to understand that I'd serve every Sunday, and on some Saturdays, I'd be working on the lawn.

He dismissed me. "Margaret will be wanting to see you."

"Yes, Father." I went into the kitchen to see Margaret.

"Ah, you're a sight for sore eyes. Sit a minute."

It was obvious that she was going to give me some cake, or cookies, and milk.

"I can only stay a minute, Margaret. I have to get ready to start my new job tomorrow."

"Ah, now, you can just sit the minute. I'll not keep you."

The milk and cake showed up to hold me in my seat.

She sat at the end of the little table. "A new job, is it?"

"Yes, it's just a messenger's job at the medical center, but it will be steady, and I'll have a little money for school at the end of the summer." I tried to eat my cake at a reasonable pace, not gobble it down.

"Well, it's a start then, isn't it?"

I knew that she'd try to prolong the conversation; she'd done it before, but I was itchy to get going.

"I gotta get going, Margaret. I'll come by to do the lawn this Saturday, or the next."

She smiled, nodded, and stood up. "You be on your way then. I'll be here."

I walked briskly toward home, with a twinge of guilt. She didn't want much from me.

It was hard to believe, but my mother insisted that my father had given up drinking.

"He's taken the Pledge," she said. "It's high time, with all the bragging he's been doing about his son becoming a priest."

"Gee, how long has this been going on?"

"Almost a month," she said. "I'm not sure which is worse, the drinking or this religious bender."

Sure enough, he came home with his pockets full of religious pamphlets. He wanted me to kneel down right then and say some prayers with him. I did it, but I kept looking over at him to see if this wasn't some kind of gag. I expected him to start laughing, but he maintained this almost scary, beatific expression the whole time.

Later, we heard on the news that the Germans had launched a new offensive in Russia. He wanted everybody to get down and pray for the Russians.

"See what I mean?" my mother said.

The great day came, and I arrived for my job wearing my best sports jacket, a medium brown wool, tan slacks, shirt and tie. After filling out some more forms and listening to a lecture on what was expected of me, to be on time, call in if sick etc.—I was escorted to my work station and introduced to Mrs. Flanagan.

The environment was very familiar to me, even as I now saw it through different eyes. I was to be stationed in the main reception area for the entire clinic building. It was a high-ceilinged room, about as big as two good-sized classrooms put together. The entrance from the street was located at the center of one of the long sides. There was a reception desk just in front of the door, and about twenty feet behind that, a line of cubicles along the wall where prospective patients were interviewed. Along the other walls, there were offices and doctors' examination rooms. The central area of the room was chock-full of long wooden benches, where patients sat to fill out forms, and to wait, and wait for their name to be called.

Mrs. Flanagan was interviewing a patient when I arrived. I was left to wait like some kind of cigar-store Indian, until she was finished. I studied her out of the corner of my eye. She looked to be about fifty, slender, a no-nonsense Irish woman with graying brown hair and rimless glasses. She finished the interview, and I was then invited behind the cubicles where Mrs. Flanagan explained my duties. I was to stand at the desk, which served as a distribution center. I would take forms and charts to the exam rooms, and charts to and from other parts of the clinic.

"You're not to sit, and don't take too long when you have to go elsewhere in the building," she said. "Sometimes you'll be asked to escort some patient, who can't find his way, to the proper clinic. Always be polite."

"Yes, ma'am."

She looked me over, seeing the actual me, I think, for the first time.

"Where do you go to school, Steven?"

"Seton Hall Prep, ma'am. It's in New Jersey."

"How nice," she said.

I took my station, standing there, trying to look inconspicuous. I didn't know whether to fold my arms, lean against the wall, or what. Most of the benches faced in my direction, and the occupants seemed to have nothing better to do than watch me. Why didn't they bring something to read?

Relief came when a secretary leaned across the desk to give me some forms and directions on how to read the codes. She was an older woman, plump with coarse skin, heavily powdered. Her perfume was awful. The codes were clear enough, there were only four places to go. I completed my first assignment in about a minute and forty-five seconds. Things got much better later in the morning, when charts started to move through the building.

Near the end of the day, the reception area was almost empty; Mrs. Flanagan called me over. "How was your first day, Steven?"

"Okay. I feel funny just standing around sometimes."

She grinned, but didn't offer any help.

"What do you study in school?"

"Oh, the usual things. And Latin."

"Well, of course. You'll be going to college, becoming a lawyer, perhaps a doctor?"

I grinned and shook my head.

"Oh," she said, "what *do* you want to be?"

I knew that she'd get it out of me sooner or later; I didn't want to play cute with her. I shrugged, "I'm studying for the priesthood."

She leaned back and gazed at me for a moment.

"Now, that's special. Your mother must be very proud."

Even before quitting time when I went back across Broadway to the bus terminal and waited to get on the old number 86, I knew I had made a mistake, telling her. I got a seat by a window on the right-hand side and, as we drove up Broadway, I looked absently at the city kids jumping rope, roller skating, and playing with tops on the sidewalks. I thought about Astoria and how good I got at spinning tops before we moved from there to New Jersey. You had to wind the string just right, a nice, even, closely spaced wind from the tip to the fat part of the top. Not too tight, or the string would skip down. I was almost famous for a short time because

I could do it faster than the other kids and keep two tops going.

We got to the stop at the entrance to the George Washington Bridge, and people jammed onto the bus. I didn't care, I was blocked into my window seat. As we crossed, I looked out over the walkway and saw barges being pulled by tugboats up the river. During earlier summers, I used to go down to the river sometimes to catch crabs, at other times just to be there. When the tugs and barges went by, I'd wave to the people who lived on the barges. There were small shacks at the back end of at least one barge in the group being towed; sometimes a small family lived there. If the kids were out playing, they'd always wave back.

I loved crossing the bridge; it was always too fast by bus. It was better to walk across the bridge; you could see straight down, and imagine how scary it would be to jump. My stomach always felt funny when I did that. If it was a nice day, and an excursion boat went under, everybody waved.

The Palisades were coming up, and I saw Bill Martin's Riviera waiting, right next to where the bridge joined the cliffs, waiting like some huge white pillbox, stark and empty. My father said that there was gambling there, even after it closed as a nightclub.

We were at the toll booths. Why did I have to tell her I was going to be a priest? She'd have those eyes on me now. If I looked at a girl cross-eyed, she'd frown and pierce me with those Irish eyes—not that I'd seen anything so far to be worried about. All the same, I had thought that I might relax a little, just for the summer.

There were seven women in my department, including Mrs. Flanagan and the secretary. They were all about the same age. By the end of the week, I'd spoken, at least briefly, to each of them. It was like working for a bunch of my aunts;

they all felt free to give me instructions, and they were all tough, not to me, but to the applicants.

They took turns in the cubicles, so that at least three out of the four cubicles were constantly busy. I stood next to the first cubicle and could hear and watch what was going on, at least for brief intervals. I couldn't decide whether Mrs. Flanagan or Mrs. Schultz gave a tougher interview.

Mrs. Schultz was big, not fat, just big. She was almost as tall as I was, she had large bones, and I'm sure she weighed more than I did. I overheard her talking to a dark-skinned woman. I couldn't tell where the woman came from.

"How can you afford that gold bracelet if you need charity medical care?"

The woman didn't hesitate one second. "Oh this," she said, glancing down at this huge hunk of gold on her wrist, "this is my sister's. I wanted to look nice today; I gotta give it back as soon as I get home."

"Do you live with your sister?"

"Oh, no. She just come by for a visit. She's from out of state."

I wanted to hang around and see how this particular contest ended, but I had charts to deliver. Probably, Mrs. Schultz wound up giving her the usual warning on the penalties for fraud and then let her pass. I knew from having been a patient there, from sitting on those long benches for hours and overhearing things, that many of these people could pay, but they knew that if they got by the first line of defense, they'd be in forever. It just took balls.

My old man must have been good at it. I'd been treated there any number of times for free. I knew that he made pretty good money, and that they would not be favorably influenced by the fact that he drank half of it before he got home. I suspect that they may have looked the other way because he was Irish. Yeah, the poor, persecuted, downtrodden Irish.

Phylis started in the cubicles during my third week; she was to take the place of women going on vacation. I knew right away that I was going to have difficulty keeping my eyes off her. She was Italian, eighteen, not pretty, but she had great breasts, and she wore blouses that were too small, causing some buttons to look strained. She was also very friendly, with a bouncy sense of humor. We got along right from the start, but I was very careful, especially when Mrs. Flanagan was around, not to hang around Phylis too much, or be caught staring at her breasts.

Late on a Friday afternoon, some of Phylis' friends came by. After work, they were going somewhere together. While they waited for Phylis, they decided to work me over. They kept it up until they made me blush. It still felt good though.

I heard a voice from behind me, "Steven!" It was Mrs. Flanagan. "These charts need to go to the third floor immediately."

"Yes, ma'am." I knew the charts couldn't be needed until Monday.

On Monday, I had a sit-down with Mrs. Flanagan.

"Steven, I've asked Phylis not to have her friends stopping by."

"Oh, I didn't mind, Mrs. Flanagan."

"Yes, well, girls will be girls. These things happen, but I'm sure that you can manage."

"It's not easy, sometimes."

"It's God's will, Steven."

Late in the afternoon, when things got slow, I tried to kid around with Phylis.

"I can't talk to you, Steven."

"Why not?" I asked. "You're not busy."

She looked over her other shoulder, like we were a couple of spies, or something.

"Because I don't want to lose my job. That's why."

I nodded and went back to my work station. The rest of the summer was starting to look like real work. The only bright spot left was a college girl who worked at the desk in 'Ear, Nose and Throat' on the fifth floor. I got to go up there twice a day. She was so beautiful that, at first, I never said anything to her, but she always smiled and said "Hi," so I started to say things to her, anything, just to talk to her for a minute. She had curly blond hair that jostled and bounced, and blue eyes. She took over my fantasy life.

One day I came by and found her talking to one of the young doctors. He left, saying something about seeing her later.

"Is that your boyfriend?" I asked.

"We're getting engaged. We'll be married next spring. I'll introduce you next time."

Right away, I felt guilty about the way I'd been thinking about her. I'd have to find a way to stop, and I knew that shoe-shining didn't work worth a damn.

CHAPTER FOUR

There were a couple of naval battles in the South Pacific that summer, which the newspapers said were a turning point in the war. The Battle of Midway was one of them. I couldn't understand how we could sink a couple of aircraft carriers, miss all of their battleships, and then say that we were now winning the war. In Europe, things made more sense; Rommel had been stopped in North Africa, and we were bombing Germany. The Russians were on our side.

People were upbeat; the complaints about shortages sounded more like joking than serious complaints. Radio shows were filled with 'Don't you know there's a war on?' humor, and *Reader's Digest* published little anecdotes revealing how ingenious our GIs could be in tweaking the enemy's nose. Some of the movies I saw made me hate the Japanese so much I couldn't wait to kill one myself, even if I was going to be a priest.

By August my whole life had settled into a dull routine; each workday followed the same pattern, and no new girls took jobs at the clinic. With the warmer weather, I picked up an additional assignment: fan adjuster. The clinic was not air-conditioned and fans were used to move the air around. The large fans in the main waiting area were mounted on stands and moved back and forth, scanning the room with a breeze. They did not reach into the area behind the cubicles so smaller fans of every size and shape were used there to keep the women cool. The problem was that they could never agree on what that meant. Some wanted the fans on them full-blast while others complained of a draft even at modest air speeds.

"Steven, I can hardly breathe. Could you get me a little more air?"

"Steven, that's too much on my back. Could you redirect it a bit?"

"Yes, Mrs. So-and-So, I'll try it again as soon as I get back from the fourth floor."

I worked at the church every other Saturday as promised, but some days I was there for less than two hours, and a half-hour of that was spent listening to Margaret. Father Paxton was rarely there; he'd come back to hear Confessions later in the afternoon. I have no idea of where he went, but according to Margaret, he wasn't doing anything of a spiritual nature.

I had heard a rumor that Paxton was going to be transferred to become pastor of a larger parish. One Saturday, after cutting the grass I was sitting at the little kitchen table eating a sandwich and drinking a glass of milk. I was going fishing after that. Margaret was going on with some complaint or another, and I wanted to change the subject.

"Margaret, I heard a rumor that Father is going to get a larger parish."

"I've heard nothing of the kind. But, you know there's them in the parish that don't particularly like him. They could be telling stories, hoping it will start something."

"Well, if he does go, he'll take you, and it will probably be easier for you."

She finished drying a pot and set it down on the old cast-iron gas stove. Then she came over, still holding the dish towel, and sat in the other chair. She sat a moment, watching me. I couldn't tell if she was going to speak, or not. I became conscious of the stillness and of the green-and-white checkered oilcloth, which covered the space between us. It was spotless, and not cracked and peeling like the red-and-white one at home.

"He'll not be taking me with him."

"Oh, sure he will. What would you do?"

She didn't answer.

"Would you retire?"

She pushed against the table top to help herself up and started to move away. "I'll retire when they're putting the dirt on my box."

I looked down at my empty plate and at the checkered oilcloth. She was old and getting frail; she wouldn't be around for much more of my life. I slugged down the rest of my milk and turned to look at her as she stood by the sink, her small back bent to her work. I could picture her little gnarled hands immersed in soapy water, scrubbing another pot. Why did she have to work so hard?

I went to her and stood just behind her. She pretended not to notice my presence. I got up my nerve and put my hand on her shoulder; it was a kind of little hug.

She kept her hands in the water. "G'wan now, the fish won't be waiting on your account."

"There are a lot of people who care about you, Margaret—especially me."

I turned and ran out the door. I managed to get around the corner before I had to wipe my eyes.

Summer vacation drew to a close; Mrs. Flanagan and the other women wished me well; Margaret sniffled a little and tried to press some money into my hands, but I absolutely refused to take it. She felt a little better when I told her how much I appreciated everything she'd already done for me, and that I would come to see her as soon as I got back home. Father Paxton surprised me when he shook my hand and gave me ten dollars; I took it.

I managed to get all my stuff into an old suitcase and a large laundry bag. My father helped me to the bus stop in Coytesville, but at the other end, I had to lug it myself. Lucky it wasn't raining.

I got my old room back, and Jenkins was my roommate. We were both pleased. But my big surprise was that I was going to be a waiter—a regular job! And I was only a sophomore! That evening everybody on the floor visited and we caught up on the news.

"Kawolski's in the Marines," somebody said, and we all told what we knew about last year's graduates.

My first setback came the next morning when I went to my class in second year Latin. The textbook looked as if it was written in a secret code. I envied the Italian kids who looked like they really enjoyed this stuff.

I figured out that I must have gotten the waiter's job because I was always so eager to do any odd job that came along, including washing priests' cars on Saturdays. They knew I needed the money. When the 'Harvest Hop' dance came along I offered to work, cleaning up tables, selling sodas, that sort of thing. It was on a Saturday night. When Jenkins left for the weekend on Friday, the last thing he said was, "Hey, Doyle, don't walk around all night at the dance with your mouth open and a hard-on."

I thanked him for his advice. Of course, I'd already been thinking about what it would be like, seeing all those girls in their fancy dresses. As the dance started I was too busy to think about it, but I did have the feeling that I was in a kind of dream world surrounded by beautiful girls; it was exciting just to be there and to see all the colors and dresses, and to hear the voices of girls all around me.

Later in the evening, I was cleaning up an empty table; one of the girls sitting nearby called to me, "Hey, waiter, bring me a Coke, will you?" She nudged her partner, I think he was a senior, and said, "Give him some money."

I wasn't there to serve people; they were supposed to get their own Cokes. I was insulted; I stared at her. God, she was good-looking.

She said, "You shouldn't look at me like that. You might get in trouble."

One of the guys at the table said, "You don't have to worry about him. He's a Church student."

Another girl laughed, "Ha, ha, ha. They're the *worst* kind." She turned to smirk at me.

Bending down, I continued to clean up.

The first girl said, "He's cute."

I was blushing, so I picked up and left. In bed that night, I couldn't get that girl out of my mind.

They say that your sophomore year is the toughest, and the longest. I can attest to that. Things just dragged; I continued in my life-and-death struggle with Latin and to maintain a positive attitude towards becoming a priest in spite of the demons inside of me. I seemed to be living in a cocoon, having virtually no contact with girls, or anyone else outside of school and associated activities.

The war provided some distractions, particularly because we now seemed to be winning. The Marines had landed on Guadalcanal, and the Army in North Africa. We finally bagged a Japanese battleship, but the Juneau had gone down with all five Sullivan Brothers. We said some special prayers for them.

Vacations were nothing to look forward to. Thanksgiving was mercifully brief, but Christmas was a disaster. The old man had given up religion and was back to the bottle. This time with a twist. He blamed me! I had been born too soon, and thereby had robbed him of his youth. He'd been saddled with a kid at the tender age of twenty-three. I had ruined him! And what was worse was the fact that I now had it too good, while he had to struggle.

He was at least partly right; there was no way I would trade the life I had at Seton Hall for one at home with him. I thought about leaving home completely, never coming home again. But he had me there. I was too young to make it on my own. Besides, I loved my mom and my sisters. I already felt guilty for not being with them more. I also knew that being there wouldn't have helped them, and may have made things worse.

I'd saved a little money and bought some presents for my family before I came home. I even had a leather key case for my father, but I had very little money left. My mother was in bed when I got home. I had to help her when she got up to hobble around and take care of the girls. She'd injured her ankle and her hip.

"Why do you always get banged up at Christmas?" I asked. "Why not wait until Easter?"

She laughed. "It's retribution for my sins," she said.

I helped with the kids, fixed their supper, got them to bed. They loved it in spite of the fact that I never took any crap from them. They did what I said, or else. It was all kind of a game, I guess, and we loved being together.

On the second day, my mother called me in. "Steven, I haven't got a cent to spare. Do you think you could go over in the woods and cut us some kind of a tree?"

I knew those woods like the back of my hand. There was

nothing that resembled a Christmas tree for miles in any direction.

"Mom, there's nothing like a Christmas tree over there."

"Steven, just any little tree. The girls won't care. At least it will be something."

"I'll get a tree," I said, without any clue as to how I'd do it.

Stealing one was out of the question—but not completely. I would have done it if it came to that. What was stealing one, very-badly-needed, Christmas tree compared to the sins I was already committing? I also thought about waiting until very late on Christmas Eve, when I might find an unsold tree, abandoned. But then I thought about all the trees at the Church. They even had extra ones that they cut up for the branches needed to decorate the crib.

After Mass the next morning, I put my problem to Father Paxton. "Father, I was wondering—my family needs a tree, and . . . "

"You haven't a tree?"

"No, Father."

He reached into his pocket for a pen, and then for his glasses. He looked around.

"Have you something to write on?"

We were in the sacristy; I searched around and came up with a blank Mass card. He took it, wrote something on it, folded it, and handed it back. I looked at it; all he'd written was his name.

"Take that," he said, "and go over to Tony Ippolito. Tell him I said to give you a tree."

"Yes, Father."

I couldn't believe it. He was commandeering a Christmas tree. Just like that! Suppose Ippolito asked me what it was for?

It was better than stealing; I gave it a go. I waited in the cold, stomping my feet until Ippolito was free. I handed him the note. "Father Paxton said that you'd give us a tree."

He didn't ask me who *us* was. Instead, he looked at the signature, which he'd probably never seen before and then squinted at me. "You an altar boy?"

I nodded, "Yes, sir."

He shuffled off and came back with a fine tree. He barely looked at me. "Here, Merry Christmas."

My mother was amazed. "How—where did you get that?"

"I stole it."

She laughed.

On Christmas morning, we gave the girls one little present each and told them they'd have to wait for the rest until Daddy got up. I went off to serve Mass, and when I got back, Mom sent the girls in to wake Daddy up. I thought he'd be pleased that I'd been able to provide a few things for Christmas. Instead, he got angry, barely civil to the girls, and he growled at me, "Big shot, heh? Think this place is cheap? Think I don't have to bust my balls for the food you eat here?"

I sat in silence, watching him. The girls were absorbed with their toys and not listening; my mother was crying. I didn't know what was coming next, whether I should be ready to run, or just wait for him to wind down.

"Santa Claus, heh?" He gestured at the girls and their toys, and then turned to me, "*We* know who Santa Claus is, don't we?" He looked down at the key case in his hand. "Santa Claus." He dropped it and walked out.

My mother, and I sat and just looked at each other until he got his coat on and left the house.

"What a shit," I said, "he can't even enjoy Christmas."

I got down on the floor to play with the girls.

I had mixed emotions when it was time to go back to school. Of course, I wanted to be away from my father, but I felt guilty about leaving my mom and sisters, especially since I'd already applied for a job as a counselor at a boys' camp for the coming summer. My mother was up and limping around, but she'd banged her eye again.

"I'm so awkward with this hip," she said. "I'm going to have to be very careful until it's healed."

The rest of the winter went well, at least for me at school. I picked up a few extra odd jobs. I bought myself a 'Prep' jacket and ran in a couple of indoor track meets. I didn't do very well, but I believed that I'd do better outdoors, in the spring, when I could stretch my legs out. The indoor tracks were too tight; I could never get going.

At Easter, I found my mother practically bubbling. She'd bought Easter bonnets and dresses for the girls, and she couldn't wait to take me out and buy me a new sports jacket and some shirts.

"What's going on?" I asked. "Are we back to religion?"

"No," she said, "he's hardly ever here! They've got him working so many hours, he's barely got enough time to sleep."

"So, he's not drinking?"

"Oh, he's drinking all right, as much as he can, but when he hits that bed, he's dead to the world. And he has no idea of how much money he's left in his pockets."

That was the best Easter we'd had for a long time.

CHAPTER FIVE

Things started to get ugly at school. Some of the older boarders, who were not Church students, began taunting a few guys about being queer. They'd yell out things like, "Hey, Ronny, are you going down tonight?" I knew what they were talking about; there had been enough dirty jokes and bull sessions in the dorm to educate anybody. But I hadn't heard of a single incident, which justified the catcalls. I tried, as best I could, to just ignore it. There were always things like that going on. The guys would get on somebody, or run some kind of 'in joke' into the ground. Whatever it was, it would die a natural death soon enough. Not this time. They kept it up.

One night, Jenkins and I got into it.

"What do you think, Doyle? These guys look like queers, or what?"

"I don't know. The guys they're ragging on are all Church students. Of course, they don't go out with girls. What do those guys expect?"

"Where there's smoke, there's fire. What about Mister Simone?"

He had a point there. I'd wondered about Simone, myself. He taught French, and was a proctor on our floor. I made allowances for him because he claimed to be practically French, and Frenchmen seemed a little odd to me, wearing berets and all that. Simone was particularly odd; he always dressed as a seminarian: black suit, white shirt, black tie. He liked to walk through the town wearing his black overcoat, hat, and a scarf; he'd smile when people said, "Good afternoon, Father." He claimed to have dropped out of the seminary because of his mother's illness, and that he would go back when she died.

"Well, Simone's kind of a screwball," I said. "That doesn't make him a queer."

"Why do you think Cary's in his room every night?"

I had no answer. At least, not at that time.

It wasn't a week later that Jenkins had to go home because of a death in his family. I had the room to myself for a couple of days. On the first night, I hopped into bed before lights-out because I had a track meet the next afternoon, and I wanted my sleep. Shoals, a senior, and one of the biggest kids in school, came into my room. His size was mostly fat, and he had a face that belonged on someone much smaller. It was narrow, and he had a small nose and eyes. With his little fuzzy mustache, he looked like a weasel.

"Hope you have all your homework done, Doyle." He gave me a playful squeeze on my knee.

"All done, Shoaly, I'm trying to get to sleep early."

"Glad to hear it. Wouldn't want you to miss any sleep." With that he reached under the blanket and grabbed my dick.

I jumped back against the wall along the inside of my bed. "CUT IT OUT," I said. Nobody had ever done that before, and, in spite of myself, I was getting a hard-on.

"Okay, okay. Just want you to know that Shoaly knows how to keep a secret."

He put one hand on my chest to hold me down and the other under the blanket. I tried to resist, or at least I like to think I did. But I was throbbing; the excitement was overpowering. It was over in a flash.

He patted my chest. "You really needed that." He smiled and left the room.

I lay there, unable to sleep.

The next day, I avoided Shoals and all the others whom I now suspected, including Mister Simone. My God! My whole life was in jeopardy. How was I going to tell this in Confession? What happens if they find out?

The taunting and the catcalls went on, and I cringed with every one. It was only a question of time. How could the priests and teachers not notice? How could they ignore the obvious implications of what they most certainly heard? Shoals became one of the prime targets. He seemed to just shrug it off, as if he didn't even hear them. God, don't let him get caught, I thought. Then I hoped that he'd do the right thing and just disappear.

As summer approached, I began to hope that the whole thing would just dwindle away, and at the end of summer, Shoals, and some others, would be gone, and the new school year would start off as if nothing had happened.

No such luck. Students were being called in to Father Harris's quarters. They refused to say a word when they came out, and then some of them were gone. No good-bye—nothing. They were just not there. Shoals was one of them.

What had happened in that room? What threats were made? What kind of pressure had been put on them? Did they tell everything?

I noticed that some students were called in who were clearly not queer. Why was that? When would my turn come?

I was never so glad to leave campus as I was that summer. Even a few weeks at home, waiting for my job to start, would be a welcome relief. Surely, it was over. Surely, in the fall, everything would be back to normal, and I could relax, not lose any more sleep worrying about what Shoals may have told them.

I spent two weeks at home waiting for my job to start at Saint Francis Camp on Culver Lake, New Jersey. It was a strange interlude; the public schools were still in session so there was nobody around. I busied myself with fishing, visits to my aunts in Fort Lee and in Manhattan, and of course, working at the church and serving Mass.

My father was still working all kinds of hours so I barely saw him, but my mother had no money. Apparently, my old man had taken to betting the ponies, and he could get rid of almost all of his money in spite of the long hours at work. My mother had bruises on her arms and neck. She told me that they had a fight when he caught her going through his pockets, and that's how it happened. I immediately asked her if that's how the other injuries had happened, but she stated very emphatically that the earlier injuries had been accidental, just as she had told me. I believed her. Looking back on it, I can't explain how I could have been so stupid; maybe the truth would have been too inconvenient for me at that time.

I loved my summer job. I was a counselor, and had my own cabin with ten boys. During the day, I was the Nature Program director; on my application, I'd told them that I'd been a Boy Scout, and had gotten a merit badge for identifying trees.

We had swimming sessions twice a day. I usually was assigned to watch the smaller kids, who swam in the 'crib,' an oversized playpen in about three feet of water. There was a resort nearby, and because of the war very few men went there. Most of the guests were secretaries from New

York City. They loved to paddle over in their canoes and check out the cute little boys. Sometimes I got up the nerve to talk with them. The head lifeguard caught me several times. "Hey, Doyle, keep your eyes on those kids," he'd yell.

Some of the older guys regularly sneaked into the resort at night. All I could do on my nights off was flirt with some of the high school girls whose families had cabins on the lake.

It was a fast summer. I had one uneventful weekend at home and was back in the dorm.

"Hey, buddy, it looks like this'll be our last year together," Jenkins said. "From the way things are shaping up, I should be out of here in time to bag me a couple of Japs or Krauts."

Jenkins was now a senior.

"Don't count on it," I said.

We talked about the war for a while. Sicily had fallen, and we'd invaded southern Italy; the Italians gave up a few days later, and things were going well in the South Pacific. The Russians were pushing the Germans back toward Germany.

"You'll be lucky to make it," I said. "Things are changing pretty fast."

"Yeah," he agreed. "And speaking of change; did you hear that Simone is not back?"

"You're kidding!"

"Uh, uh. *And,* Murphy says that Father Reed is gone to. You heard about him, right?"

I remembered some rumor about Reed picking up a hitchhiker in south Jersey, and then trying to make him. The kid turned out to be a Seton Hall student, and, the story goes, he squealed to his parish priest. I wasn't much interested in Reed; what concerned me was that it might not be over, as I thought.

"That's the last of it though, wouldn't you think?" I said.

"I doubt it," he said. "There's a couple of guys, and one or two teachers, that look pretty queer to me."

"Aw, just because a guy's not married, or he acts a little different, doesn't mean he's queer."

"You think so? You'll see. The 'Great Homo Hunt' isn't over."

That's all I needed to hear. And he was right; within a couple of weeks the investigations started, and two students and one teacher were gone. Rumors flew, even implicating two more priests. I just wanted it to be over, but nothing happened to involve me, and school life went along as always until a few weeks before Thanksgiving.

It was about ten minutes before lights-out; I was brushing my teeth in the fourth floor john. Jenkins had just left, and I was worrying about my Latin test the next morning. Maybe I could get up early and get in a little more studying before breakfast. And maybe, I could finish early in the dining room. And maybe, I should cut first period Algebra to get in more studying.

I spotted him in the mirror; I had no idea of how long he'd been standing there, watching me make faces in the mirror. The very private Mister Warren, who had the only living quarters on the fourth floor, just across from the john, stood in the doorway. I spit out and turned to face him, fully expecting to be bawled out for making too much noise before Jenkins left. He was in his shirtsleeves; the only time I ever saw him, before or since, without his three-piece brown suit, complete with gold watch chain and some kind of society key.

He spoke, "Doyle, you use this toilet frequently, do you not?"

"Yes, Mister Warren."

"I wonder. Are you ever up here during the day?"

"Sometimes, if it's crowded downstairs."

He nodded and looked off, making no move to come into the room. "I'd like you to do me a favor." He paused a moment while I nodded my assent and then continued, "I'd like you to keep an eye open for anyone who doesn't belong up here—any strangers."

"I will, Mister Warren."

He smiled—a rare thing for him. It wasn't really a smile—more like a crack in his face. "I'll be very appreciative," he said, turning away.

I just made it past Mister Fagan's open door before lights-out. I lay in bed with my eyes open; my mind flipping between worrying about my Latin test and my new status with Mister Warren.

I struggled through the Latin test just before lunch and then waited on tables, stuffed down some lunch, cleared the dishes, and made it to History two minutes late. Mister Howell gave me his usual forced smile as I took my seat. It wasn't until after school that I felt that I could take a break. I popped into Freddy Joyce's room and sat on his bed. He set his magazine aside. "Don't you have track practice?"

"Yeah," I said, "I've got time."

He shrugged. I told him about Warren.

"He's probably another homo." Freddy said. "You better watch it."

I considered this; Freddy was always so much more knowledgeable about these things than I was. "You think so?"

"Sure. I'm not saying I *know*, but he never hangs out with the other teachers. He's always going off somewhere by himself. And that room—the only one on the top floor. I'd stay out of there if I were you."

Freddy was sticking a pin in my balloon; I thought maybe Warren was just lonesome, or maybe just needed someone to exchange a few words with, or maybe, somebody was stealing from his room, and he needed help. I got up to leave. "I'll see how it goes."

"Keep me posted," Freddy said, picking up his magazine.

I had no further contact with Warren that day or the next, but I did make it a point to get to the fourth floor a couple of times during school hours. It seemed that at just about any time there were kids who had a free period, and some of them went to the fourth floor john to play cards and smoke. I decided to report this fact to Warren. I made a quick trip to the fourth floor just before evening study hall started at seven o'clock. I found Warren just leaving his room.

"Thank you, Steven." I felt as if I'd just been promoted; it wasn't 'Doyle'; it was 'Steven.' "I wasn't concerned with students," he said, "more with people who don't belong on campus." Another smile for me. "And please don't mention this to anyone else."

I nodded, "Right," and turned to go. He locked his door. One, two, three, four!

Four locks?! At the top of the stairs, I glanced back; he was headed the other way.

CHAPTER SIX

The next day was Friday, my one day to really goof off after class and a very quick track workout. I took my shower, dressed and went down the hall looking for somebody else who was staying on campus for the weekend. I found Vinny Carpatsi. He had a football game the next day; his father would take him home after that. Vinny was a senior but a really neat guy; we did some stuff together, especially when he was around for part of a weekend. "Feel like going down for a soda?" I asked.

Vinny looked me over, as he sometimes did—probably trying to think of something clever to say.

"Should be some girls down at the Cricklewood," I said.

"Is that right, Father Doyle? Perhaps we should go down and convert a few of them." He was grinning and getting his jacket on. Vinny knew that I was no longer serious about becoming a priest, but that I had to keep up the pretense in order to stay in school.

We walked diagonally across the broad lawn to the corner of the campus and crossed South Orange Avenue. The Cricklewood was on the opposite corner. Every booth along the walls was filled with girls, except two where half the occupants were boys.

All the tables in the center of the room were empty; the jukebox blasted away at the other end, but no one was dancing. We sat down at the center table; Vinny looked relaxed, but I was struggling to look casual and not to knock anything over. I ordered my once-a-week treat, a chocolate malted; Vinny got a black and white sundae.

Vinny spotted somebody he knew, and I followed him over to a booth filled with girls. I stood just behind him and to the side as he exchanged a few words with one of the girls. Then one of the girls climbed over a friend to get out of the booth. She stood in front of me and put her index finger on my chest. My mouth must have been hanging open; I had no idea of what was going to happen next. "I've seen you running around in your underwear," she said. The booth exploded with giggles. Vinny was grinning at me.

I tried to laugh—my throat was too dry. I cleared my throat. "That's my track uniform," I said.

"Oh," she said. "I thought maybe they ran out of uniforms, and you had to run in your underwear."

They were all laughing now. Finally, I relaxed and had a good laugh, myself. The next thing I knew, Vinny was sandwiched into one side of the booth, and I was on the other side. The waitress brought over our orders. I felt the heat and softness of girls bodies on both sides of me; I could barely taste my malted. Maybe one of these girls would take me home to an empty house and seduce me before supper.

The girls were all from South Orange High. Normally, they stayed in town but decided on a walk because it was Friday and a nice day. Most of them had never met boarding students from the Prep before, and there were very few day-hop students living in South Orange. Most of the residents were WASPS, or at least it seemed that way to us. We were told to set a good example in town—never cut up in South Orange.

They were curious. Vinny told them about our daily routine, and then about some of our eccentric priests and teachers. He told them about Captain Bly, other wise known as Father Riley, the Dean of Discipline. Then he threw the conversation to me. "Doyle, here, almost got us expelled last year for a water fight he organized."

They all turned to me. "Yeah, the Captain made us pay for that one. Took us half the night to clean up, and then he fined us a buck each. It wouldn't have been so bad except that the month before we got blamed for turning on the fire hose—just a little bit, so that it would uncoil like a big snake during the night."

The girls were fascinated; I felt like the most charming guy in town. I went on. "That's nothing. Last month we found a guy taking a nap late in the afternoon. We spread some lighter fluid and some papers around his bed and lit them up. Then we jumped up and down yelling FIRE! FIRE!" I looked around for approval. They turned to Vinny. "Is he making this up?"

He waited until they were all focused on him, and then he glanced across at me. "Is it all right to tell them the truth, do you think?" I grinned, curious to see how he was going to top me. "Well," he said, "Steven, here is a special student. We never let him go anywhere by himself, if you follow my meaning." They all turned back to me; I wasn't sure what their expressions were saying, but nobody moved away, and I thought it was pretty funny.

Our glasses were all empty; Vinny and I exchanged glances. "I don't get paid until next week," I said to no one in particular. "We'll buy sodas," one of the girls said. I don't know how I got down another malted, but I did. When it was time to go, Marion said, "I live just beyond the other side of the campus, behind the gym. Can you walk me home?" Vinny walked with the others back toward town.

Vinny saw me at supper. "Doyle, you devil you. What happened?"

"I'm bringing her to the game tomorrow."

"I hope nobody sees you," he said, referring to my status as a Church student.

"There's no rule against it," I said.

The game started at one-thirty; I left to pick up Marion right after lunch. She lived in a two-story gray house, about two blocks away from the back end of the campus. I was introduced to her mother and her grandparents, who lived in the same house; her father was away in the Merchant Marine. I was nervous, but I got through all that okay. What really worried me was the possibility of bumping into one of the priests at the game.

It was a home game, and there were several priests there: Father Cochran, and four or five others whom I didn't recognize—probably alumni. It was easy to avoid them. A number of my day student friends said 'hi' and gave Marion a curious once-over. I knew that if I was going to keep going out with her, I'd have to clue her in about the Church student business.

It was a glorious fall day, and very warm for November. Marion wore a yellow pullover sweater and a light brown cardigan; which she did not button. She had on a dark brown pleated wool skirt with knee socks to match. Everything except her saddle shoes was coordinated to go with her brown eyes, her hair, and with the season of the year. I had on a regular white cotton shirt, a tan sleeveless pullover sweater, blue pants, and a maroon corduroy sports jacket. My blue jacket would have been a better color, but the sleeves were noticeably too short.

I got Marion a Coke and we sat high up in the stands. She sat close on my right and leaned against my shoulder.

That was nice; I wasn't sure if I was supposed to do anything, or not. I didn't want to flub my first real date. I looked down through the stands to see what other guys were doing with their girls. Of course, I had no idea of how well they knew their girls; they could have been going steady. Marion took my hand. That was a good sign; maybe I could put my arm around her later, or at least try it on the way home.

As the game went on, and things got exciting, we stood up; Marion hugged my arm. Good God! I thought I could feel her breast. During the second half, I did put my arm around her; it was nice, but not as thrilling as feeling what I thought was her breast against my arm.

Bloomfield did it to us again, 28 to 7. Normally I would have cared, but that day all I could think about was Marion. After the game, we went for sodas, and then I walked her home. She was a little short for me, so it was awkward to walk with my arm around her waist, but I managed. "I'd like to see you again," I said. She leaned against me, looked up and smiled. "I can only get out on Friday and Saturday nights," I said, "and I have to be back in by eleven."

"That's okay." She put an arm around my waist. I decided that I'd tell her about being a Church student some other time. At her front door, she got up on her toes to give me a hug and a kiss on the cheek. "You're sweet," she said.

I walked back onto the campus still feeling the warm glow of Marion. I tried to form a good mental picture of her, so that I could fantasize later. It wasn't easy; somehow, the details of her face eluded me. I concentrated on the brief feeling of her breast against my arm. Even that wasn't a clear recollection.

That evening, after supper, I went looking for someone who might want to go to the movies, but everyone had either gone home, or was already out somewhere. I decided to get a leg up on my homework for a change, instead of leaving it all for Sunday night. I didn't get much done.

I wanted a girl friend; I'd been thinking about it for long enough—all the while behaving in every way as if I had a vocation for the priesthood. Was Marion going to be my girl? Could I wind up marrying her? This was scary stuff. If she wanted me, I knew I couldn't resist her. If the priests found out, I'd have to give her up, and swear off girls, or leave school.

By Sunday afternoon, I'd made a plan: I'd ask Marion to help me to keep her a secret. At the end of the school year, I'd fess up to the headmaster, Father Harris. I'd ask him to let me come back on some basis as a regular student for my last year at the Prep. I called Marion to ask her for a date on the following weekend. She said that we could go to a small party at a friend's house.

It was cold; I picked her up at seven. Her mother smiled at me and said that we should have a nice time. I think she liked the idea that Marion would be back home before eleven o'clock. We were both bundled up against the cold and we moved quickly along the tree lined streets with Marion holding onto my arm. The night was dark and windy, but street lights showed the way and the newly bare trees cast swaying shadows along the sidewalks.

"I hope your friends won't mind us leaving so early," I said.

"Oh, they won't mind," she said. "They'll have more privacy."

"Privacy?"

She grinned and hugged my arm. "You'll catch on."

We got to her friend's house; it was big. I was beginning to get a queasy feeling in my stomach; I'd never been in such a rich looking place before. Joan, her friend, took us in to meet her parents, the Carlsons. They were seated in a large, very elegant, living room listening to some news on the radio. They were dressed as if they were going out, or had just come in. Mr. Carlson was a tall, pretty handsome guy; he was interested to hear that I was a student at the Prep. He shook my hand, and I could see, and smell, that he was slightly drunk.

It was a skill I developed before I became a teenager; I could quickly tell if my father, my uncles, or anyone else for that matter, was cold sober, medium drunk, or blotto. Actually, women were more difficult; I noticed that Mrs. Carlson had remained seated.

The party was in their finished basement. We were the fourth, and last couple to arrive. The others were gathered around the bar, drinking Cokes and making loud conversation all about some other kids at South Orange High. The guys were talking. "Yeah, lucky we had Wally with us. These kids from Harrisburg really wanted a fight." "Yeah, nobody messes with Wally."

I was introduced and tried to make some kind of neutral conversation. The other guys quickly went back to showing off for the girls. Marion pulled on my arm. "Let's dance," she said, taking me way over to the other side of the room. I knew it. My dancing was right up there with my Latin; we should have gone to the movies. She put on a record. Thank God, it was at least a slow one.

There'll be blue birds over the white cliffs of Dover
Tomorrow, just you wait and see.

"Oh, no!" one of the guys yelled. "I'm gonna fall asleep."

"Don't be such a jerk," Joan said, making him dance with her.

I was moving around, stiff legged, holding Marion about ten inches away. "Don't be shy," she said, pulling me in. I was in trouble; not only could I not dance, but I got an instant hard-on. I tried to bend over a little bit to keep my hips away, but she kept bumping into it. "I have to go to the bathroom," I said. She took my hand and led me. "It's right in there."

"I'll only be a minute." I closed the door and opened my pants. I looked at it and knew that it wasn't going to go down. I looked around for something to tie it with—nothing. Finally, I took some toilet paper, wadded it up, put in front and pulled up my shorts as high and as tight as I could get them. I tightened my belt to hold up the shorts and went back out. One of the couples had disappeared. Marion and I sat at the bar for a few minutes. What a relief! Then she wanted to dance. "I never learned to jitterbug," I said. "Could you teach me some steps?" I poured myself into the lesson.

About a half-hour later, the missing couple showed up, acting kind of quiet. Marion put on a slow record. I thought I could do better this time. We danced over to a door leading to another part of the basement. She took my arm. "We can be alone in here," she said.

"I can't see," I said.

"Your eyes will get used to it," she said.

My hard-on was back. She had expectations. I had no idea of how far they went. I felt the top of her head against my jaw; her arms were sliding inside my jacket, around my waist. I held her close and kissed her. She was squirming around and trying to get her tongue in my mouth. I could hardly breathe. She turned around and held my arms around her waist. I felt her buttocks against my thighs; I knew that I had less than a minute left before I popped. She took my wrists and slid my hands up to her breasts. That did it. I just held on—what a mess. Thank God for the toilet paper.

She wanted more; she was unbuttoning her blouse. This was great; I could be a little calmer now. The lights flashed on, and quickly off. "Hey you guys. Time's up." It was Irene, one of the other girls. I was relieved that it wasn't Mr. Carlson. Marion stood behind me to button up her blouse, and we went out to sit at the bar.

We left shortly after and walked slowly back to her house. Not much was said. At her front door, I kissed her and said, "Marion, I know you're going to say that I'm crazy, but I'm sure that I'm in love with you."

She kissed me back in a very serious way, and I floated back to my room.

The next day, Sunday, I tried to study, but Marion kept crowding into my mind. I had an all-day hard-on. It was getting close to Thanksgiving, which I now began to think of as an exile from Marion. I had to see her at least one more time although just going to the movies would seem pretty tame.

CHAPTER SEVEN

I ran into Mr. Warren that night in the upstairs hallway; he was just undoing all his locks. "Ah, Steven, I haven't seen you for a while."

"No, sir. I've been keeping busy."

"I imagine that you're going home for Thanksgiving?" He sure sounded cheerful—a few nips?

"Yes, sir."

"And where would that be?"

"Coytesville."

He looked at me, waiting for some kind of explanation, like 'It's between Brazil and Colombia.'

"It's part of Fort Lee," I explained.

"Ah, up on the Palisades; should be well away from the war up there."

"Actually," I said, "there's an FBI listening station just up the street from where I live."

"Really? What do they listen for?"

I shrugged. "I don't know. They've got all kinds of radio stuff, and some special radio cars."

"In Fort Lee?"

"Coytesville."

He undid the last lock and went into his room.

That Saturday night, the last before Thanksgiving, I took Marion to the movies. "Come on in," she said when we got to her house. It was early; her grand parents were still up so we stayed in the kitchen. Her mother offered us some cookies and milk and left us alone. Marion was in a cuddly mood, but I was nervous as a cat; I could hear people moving around in the living room. At one point, her grand father came in for a glass of water, looking me over and giving me a big smile while he was at it. I said to Marion, "It sure would be nice to be alone with you—really alone."

She put an arm around me and stabbed me in the chest with her breast. "Yes, that would be really nice. Maybe you could find someplace?"

She let me go, and I struggled to think and keep from getting a hard-on at the same time. Where? Where could I possibly take her? I was hoping that she'd come up with something. Her mother came in to remind me of the time. "So you won't get in trouble." I wondered if she was trying to tell me something.

I couldn't get to sleep; I got up to walk around the halls. Out of curiosity, I went up to the fourth floor. The lighting was dim, making the shiny floor and dark painted doors look like a spooky movie. It was so quiet that I could easily hear my soft slippers swooshing along the floor. There was a light coming from under the door to Mr. Warren's room. I paused for just a second to listen. There was some kind of noise; I couldn't make it out, but I didn't want to stay there. I moved along. The next door was the entrance to a janitors supply room. I tried the door; it opened quietly and in the dim light coming from a small window I saw the room's simple contents: some cans of soaps and waxes, mops, brooms, and an old couch. I went back to my room.

On Sunday afternoon, Marion and I went for a walk. We went to the park, which was near the campus behind the athletic field. It was not a nice day, cold, overcast, and a little windy. We had the park to ourselves. "I guess I won't see you again until after Thanksgiving," I said.

"That's too bad," she said. Her tone sounded a little detached. "I hope you have a nice holiday."

"I don't really have a choice," I said. "They make everybody go home for Thanksgiving."

She nodded and leaned against me.

"Maybe I could come back early on Sunday."

"That would be nice," she said.

We stopped at a bench that was sheltered from the wind by some high bushes. We sat down and I kissed her. She snuggled against me and pulled on me. I slipped my hand under her jacket. She kissed me. "We can't do much here," she said, putting her hand on my thigh. At that point, we didn't *need* to do much; I was flying. She got up and pulled me along. I had this feeling of desperation; I had no access to a car, no money. I had already told her about being a Church student, attending the Prep on the cuff, and my clothes told her everything else she needed to know. What did I have to lose? "I couldn't sleep last night," I told her. "I went walking around the halls." I hesitated.

"*And?*"

"I found this, kind of a closet, on the fourth floor."

"A closet?" She sounded interested, as if we were getting into some kind of conspiracy.

"Actually, it's a small room. The janitor keeps some stuff in there. It was unlocked."

We walked in silence.

"And you think you could sneak me in there?" she said.

"It's just an idea."

"What happens if we get caught?"

"To you? Probably nothing."

"And to you?" she asked.

"I wouldn't be able to see you for a while. They might suspend me."

She stopped and held me tightly. Her concern made me almost cry. "I wouldn't want that to happen," she said. "But it does sound exciting."

We developed our plan. Her grandparents went to bed around nine-thirty; her mother worked at a local defense plant from four till midnight. If Marion got home before twelve-thirty, she'd be okay. I would meet her at the basement door twenty minutes after lights-out, at ten-twenty. I'd lead her up the stairs; if I got caught, I'd say I was going to the toilet, and she would sneak out. If she got caught, she'd say that Ronny Stump told her to meet him. Ronny had left school a few days earlier. I was sure they'd just let her go. They sure didn't need any more sex scandals at that point.

We set it up for Monday night. I've never been so nervous in my life; I could barely eat any supper, and studying was impossible. I wanted to call it off, but that would have been the end of Marion. Where would I ever find another girl like her; she was a sex goddess dropped from the blue. I actually found myself praying for no problems. Maybe, Marion wouldn't show, and I could just collapse into bed. The time ticked away, getting faster after lights-out.

I put on my bathrobe and slippers and sneaked down the hall, past Mr. Fagan's open door. I stopped at the landing to listen and then ran down each flight of stairs. The basement was like a tomb; I could hear myself breathing. I opened the latch; the sound reverberated from the steel staircase and the concrete walls and floor. I listened for a second and then opened the door a crack. Marion slipped through. We went to the bottom of the first flight of stairs. I went up, listened and waved to Marion. I went ahead, and we repeated the process. On the third floor, the dormitory floor, I could easily see the light from Mr. Fagan's open door.

I motioned to Marion and ran up to the fourth floor where I stood in the dark, holding my breath. I heard a sound, but Marion was already at my side. It must have been Mr. Fagan closing his door.

I grasped Marion's hand and kissed her forehead. We went down the hall. There was that light coming from under Mr. Warren's door; we didn't stop. I'd checked the janitor's door earlier; it opened quietly. Inside, I took a couple of deep breaths. Marion giggled. "Shusss, Mr. Warren is right next door." She nodded.

We stood for a moment, letting our eyes adjust to the dark and then moved over to the couch. I had been so worried about getting this far that I'd given little thought to what would happen next. Apparently, Marion *had* thought about it. After we sat down on the couch, I hadn't even kissed her when she started to remove her jacket and then her blouse. She stopped there; I think she wanted me to do the rest. I knew that when that bra came off, I would come for the first time that night. I didn't care, there was plenty of time, and I didn't care about being caught either.

A little while later, she whispered, "Uh, uh. Please don't take them off." She referred to her panties. Still later, "We can't go all the way."

"Right." I had just enough breath to say that.

A strange sound came from Warren's room. We stopped to listen; it was a squealing sound.

"Is that a radio?" she whispered.

I listened. Sure enough, a radio. "Sounds like a real cheap one," I whispered.

We listened for another minute and then went back to what we'd come there for. After what seemed like the shortest of times, she whispered, "It's time for me to go." I kissed her and kissed her. Watching her put her clothes back on was almost as sexy as seeing them come off. Everything was dark and quiet when we slipped back down the stairs, and I latched the door after Marion.

I was surprised when I woke up the next morning feeling refreshed after so little sleep. Sex had to be good for you. I felt different after that. I knew that I hadn't actually gotten laid, but it seemed awfully close. How much better could 'going all-the-way' be? I spent a lot of time thinking about Marion, but I managed to do some real studying too. On Wednesday, the last day before vacation, I was in no hurry to leave. I called Marion one last time to tell her how much I was going to miss her, and to plan another rendezvous. She seemed willing enough. What did she see in me? It was a question I'd answer, but not until years later.

After calling Marion, I was on my way back upstairs to get my bag and go home when Mr. Warren stopped me. "Steven, I wonder if you'd give me a hand with a box?" I followed him to his room where he went through the lock business. He invited me in. The room was narrow in the distance from the door to the group of windows on the opposite side, but it was a long room with a bed and reading chair near the right hand wall and book shelves on the left hand side, the wall next to the janitor's closet. In front of the windows, which provided plenty of light, there was a work table. The windows also afforded a great view of the entire front side of the campus, including the tree lined driveway, which wound its way up to the fronts of our building, the adjacent Administration building and Chapel.

Mr. Warren pointed to a wooden box sitting on the table. He picked up a loose radio speaker and set it on top of the box. Together, we carried the box down to his car, which was parked right next to the basement door. As we put it in the back, I asked, "This is pretty heavy. Is it a radio?"

"Uh, yes it is, Steven. I'm having it repaired."

"Wow. Why don't you get the guy to come here?"

Mr. Warren covered the radio and speaker with a blanket and then reached into his pocket. He handed me fifty cents. "It's an old radio; I'm not sure the local shop would have parts for it. I have a friend, who's confined to a wheelchair, but he does great work." He leaned close. "And he's very inexpensive."

I nodded my understanding.

"Have a nice Thanksgiving," he said. "And, mum's the word."

CHAPTER EIGHT

In Coytesville, I was still known as that good Catholic kid who went off to become a priest. Father Paxton was still the pastor and only priest at Holy Trinity; he assumed that I'd be delighted to serve at seven-thirty Mass every morning except Sunday, when he had me down for the ten o'clock Mass. I felt like some kind of prize animal on display, and something like an impostor at the same time. The kids I used to hang around with all had new friends from whatever high schools they were attending, and I sure didn't know any girls that I could call up. I looked up Mickey Fallon, who had been in Scouts with me, and he got me invited to a house party on Saturday night.

There was something I had to take care of on Saturday afternoon; I had to get to Confession. After what I'd been doing with Marion there was no way that I could risk going to Confession at Seton Hall, and I sure wasn't going to go to Father Paxton. I got out my bike and rode down to Fort Lee, to Madonna Parish; hardly any priest would know me there. I hated Confession, going in and telling a priest that you'd done these things that were so depraved, telling him that you couldn't resist sexual urges of the most shameful type. And you had to tell him exactly what you'd done—no weasel words like 'sins of the flesh.' I had an extra problem that Saturday; I knew that at the end, the priest would make me promise not to see that girl again.

I got to the church and went inside. There were two priests hearing Confessions and both lines were short. One part of me said to just plunge in and get it over with. I couldn't. Why was I going through this exercise? I knew that I'd be committing these same sins again, even getting laid, if possible. Wouldn't it be better to do nothing? I thought about serving Mass the next day; Father Paxton would surely notice if I didn't take Communion, and I couldn't do that without being absolved of my sins, being forgiven by God through his agent, the priest. Maybe I *wouldn't* see Marion again—maybe she'd be run over by a truck. I went to Confession.

I took my time with the preliminaries, the 'Bless me Father, for I have sinned' part. All the while my mind was spinning with the various terms and phrases I'd chosen to describe my sins. "There's this girl, Father. I've been dating her, and we—well we.."

He interrupted. "Have you had carnal knowledge of this girl?"

Carnal knowledge? What was he talking about?

"Well, Father . . . "

"Just tell me, son."

"We didn't go all-the-way."

"I see. Is it necessary for you to see this girl frequently, in school, for example?"

"No, Father."

When I got out of the Confessional, I went straight to the door. I'd say my penance later. What a relief! It was over; all I had to do was keep Marion out of my mind—at least for a while.

I knew about a half dozen of the guys and two or three girls at the party, but after they asked me a few questions about Seton Hall, they lost interest in me and went back to talking about their own lives. I just hung around listening in. After a while, Mickey came over and took me aside. "No girls at your school, huh?"

"Right. Theoretically, we're supposed to learn more without having them around."

He sniggered. "Does it work?"

"Not for me."

"So, are there any around? Can you get a date?"

"Sure, I've had dates."

He nodded. "You guys must get horny though?"

"And you don't?"

He laughed. "Speaking of which . . . " He gestured with his head at a blond who had just entered the room. "Check those boobs."

I did, until she looked my way. I turned back to Mickey. "Nice," I said.

"You get laid yet?"

"Well, not exactly. How about you?"

"Oh, yeah," he said. "You know my motto: Find 'em, feel 'em, fuck 'em, and forget 'em."

I guess he thought that was pretty clever, and that I'd not heard it before. I forced a smile; I could never laugh at those kinds of jokes. I simply could not imagine doing it with some girl that I didn't have real feelings for. The thought of it being some kind of sport, where the girl loses, made me nauseous. But I wanted to fit in.

"Where do you get your rubbers?" I asked.

The question caught him off guard, and I immediately realized that he'd been putting me on. I was disappointed because I really wanted to acquire some rubbers.

"Oh, I don't get them myself. They don't sell them to kids. My buddy's big brother gets them."

I nodded. There wasn't much point in asking him to sell me a couple, but I did anyway.

"I just got one," he said. "I can't spare it." He moved off to talk to someone else.

I wandered around and amazed myself when I struck up a conversation with the blond. I concentrated on her eyes, which were blue.

"I hardly know anyone here," she said.

I would have thought otherwise from the guys crowding around her. "I'm away at school," I said. "I don't usually hang out with these kids."

"We just moved into town," she said, looking at me and somehow excluding the ring of guys.

"Nice party?"

She didn't say anything.

"You don't care for it?"

She shook her head. "Some of the things they talk about . . . And the language.." She shook her head again.

"Did you come with somebody?" I glanced around to see if one of her entourage was going to step out and claim her.

"No one important. I'm leaving." She had a cool, self-confident expression on her face, which I now noticed was very pretty.

I don't know where I got the nerve. "I'd be pleased to walk you home."

"That's okay; I don't live very far from here."

"Unless you say no, I'd really like to walk you home." Wow! It just came out, smooth as can be.

She smiled. I couldn't be falling in love again this soon. We found our coats. Mickey Fallon watched us leave. I wish that I could have taken a picture of his expression.

Her house was on Linwood Avenue, only a half mile from

where I lived. The party was on Fourth Street, so we had to cross the highway and head up past P.S. #3. As soon as we started our walk, she asked me, "You go to a prep school. Is that right?"

"Yes, Seton Hall."

"So you're a Catholic?"

"That's right."

She looked directly at me, almost teasingly. "A good one?"

I had to laugh; I had no idea of what the right answer was. "Most of the time," I said.

She smiled and linked her arm around mine, pulling me toward her. "So am I," she said. "And, I'm always good." She grinned widely, enjoying her own joke.

I was so amazed at the feel of her breast against my arm—there was no doubt about it this time, that I couldn't think of what to say.

"Were those boys at the party Catholics?" she asked.

"Some of them are."

She didn't comment. We talked about other things. "We moved here from Evanston, Illinois a month ago," she said. "My father works for the FBI."

"No kidding. Does he work at that big house on Linwood? The one with all the radio stuff?"

"No. He knows some of those men, but he works in New York."

She asked me about Seton Hall, and what kind of things I did there besides go to school. I told her about being on the track team. She said that her father had been on the track team at Notre Dame. She said that he still held the school record for the half mile. I was impressed, and I guess it showed.

We got to her house, too soon by me. We stood on the porch at least two feet apart. "What Mass are you going to?" she asked.

"Father Paxton has me down to serve the ten o'clock."

She smiled, her hands holding together in front of her thighs. "I usually go earlier," she said, "so that I won't starve."

She was telling me that she usually went to Communion, which required a fast until after the Mass.

"What time do you have to leave for school?"

"Right after lunch," I said.

She nodded.

I said, "Sometimes, there's not much time."

She shrugged and held out her hand.

Slowly, I took it, thinking madly. "I'll be home for Christmas." It was really a question.

She smiled. "That's nice."

"I could write," I said out of desperation, wondering if I sounded as pathetic as I felt.

She smiled again, very broadly this time. "That sounds like fun."

And that's how I met Irene McNally.

The next morning I very piously held the golden tray under her chin as she received Communion at the ten o'clock Mass. She waited for me outside. As I walked her home, I realized that I was seeing her in daylight for the first time. She wore no make-up, except perhaps for a little lipstick; her skin was as clear and smooth as a baby's with a natural glow at her cheeks. She dressed modestly, but there was no denying those boobs. And she was tall, just right for me. I began to imagine what it would feel like to hold her if we were dancing. I stopped myself; we'd both just been to Communion.

We didn't talk much. I walked as if in a dream; never before had I had the exclusive attention of a girl as good-looking as she was. And it wasn't just me; those guys at the party had been drooling over her. I wanted so very badly to make a solid impression, and yet, at the same time, a little voice inside warned me protect myself; told me that it couldn't last. Surely, some handsome guy with a car, with money, would take her from me like candy from a baby. We got to her porch; I tried to be reserved, not to overplay my hand. She looked at me, a question in her eyes. I couldn't hold back, I blurted it out. "I'll die if I don't see you again, and Christmas is a hundred years away."

She smiled and reached for my hand. "We can write. You said that you'd write. And we can send each other a picture."

"I don't have anything good," I said.

"They're never any good," she said. "Send it anyway."

She put her hand up to my cheek. I held it there for a second, and then she went inside.

After lunch, I packed my bag and said good-by to my sisters. My mother was in the kitchen; I went in to say good-by. She handed me a bag of food, mostly cookies. "We'll see you at Christmas."

I looked at her, really for the first time that vacation. I'd been so wrapped up in worrying about Confession, about Marion, and then with my new love, Irene, that I hadn't spent any real time with my mother. She looked okay if you didn't look real close. Her eyes always looked a little dreary from lack of sleep.

"Has anything else happened with Pop?" I asked.

"Just the usual. Sometimes I wish that the Army would take him."

"Isn't he too old? And with three kids?"

She sat at the kitchen table peeling some potatoes. She stopped and gazed off. "They're taking fathers with one kid. But, you're right; they won't get to him before the war is over." She went back to peeling.

I stood there not knowing what to say or how to bring the conversation to an end. Finally, I asked, "Why don't you leave him?"

She looked at me for what felt like a long time, and then she said, "You're still young, Steven, too young to understand." She got up, wiping her hands on her apron, and put her hands on my shoulders. She turned me around. "Off you go, and don't be worrying about me."

Off I went, wondering if I'd bump into the old man staggering home from Gus Becker's saloon. As I passed P.S. #3, I relaxed. I'd spent three happy years in that school. It was the last place where I'd really fit in. Some of the other kids came from big families, had drunks for fathers, some of those fathers even beat up their mothers. Probably some of those fathers had been drafted; the family allotment check would come straight home making life better than ever before. My father was a little too old, and he had a defense job and three kids. Too bad.

God! The playground looked small. I remembered when it had been a big deal to be able to hit a ball over the fence into Mrs. Zwicker's yard. She'd keep the ball, unless a kid was fast enough to get in and out without being caught, in which case she'd complain to the principal. She had a nice yard, lots of flowers. She paid kids twenty cents an hour for yard work, and she worked them like galley slaves. You had to be pretty hard-up to go and ask for work at Mrs. Zwicker's. She was interesting to talk to though; she used to take in boarders. In the old days, before the movies relocated to California, several large studios were located in Fort Lee. Some of the stars, like Fatty Arbuckle, stayed with her, and she knew others like Mary Pickford and Gilbert Roland.

CHAPTER NINE

I got back to Seton Hall a little after five, much later than I had promised Marion; I needed to call her. I started up the stairs to put my bag away. Mister Warren was waiting on the second floor; he must have seen me coming up the driveway

"Steven, I wonder if, after you've put your bag away, you'd help me with a box."

"Sure, Mister Warren. Is the radio fixed already?"

"No, this is just some books."

I helped him with the box and left immediately, to show him that I didn't expect a tip. Besides, the box weighed just about as much as the radio had. I wondered if maybe it was too old to be fixed, and he just didn't want to talk about it. I went downstairs to call Marion.

"My mother was very late with the lunch," I said. "I don't think she wanted me to leave."

"I've been waiting all afternoon," she said.

"I'm sorry; it's not because I didn't miss you." I went on to ask her to the movies that Friday.

She agreed, and then she asked, "Do we have to wait that long?"

I knew that there was only one answer. "No," I said, wishing that I'd planned this call a little better. I'd been thinking about Irene, and also thinking that it would be a good idea to avoid committing a Mortal Sin for at least one more week. I knew that I was a complete hypocrite; I just needed a little room for rationalization. "I was hoping to see you soon," I said.

"I can do it tomorrow," she said.

"Wonderful."

That Monday, I worried less about being caught. It wasn't so much that I was getting used to the routine of sneaking Marion into the building, but that the consequences of getting caught seemed less drastic now that I'd completely accepted the fact that I had no intention of becoming a priest. I wasn't completely happy about seeing Marion either. It was one thing to give up on becoming a priest because I couldn't live without girls, and another thing to sink into a life of depravity. Why was I so weak? How would the whole thing end if I couldn't resist an opportunity, even a risky one to fondle a girl's breasts?

We repeated our procedure exactly as before, getting to the fourth floor closet without any mishaps. As soon as we got inside, we realized that it was darker than last time. It was overcast; no moonlight came through the dusty window. Even after our eyes adjusted, we could hardly see. It took some careful feeling along the shelves to get to the couch. There were some loose boards laying on it, which we removed as quietly as we could. Finally, it was time to do what we'd come for. The darkness had a strange effect on both of us I think we were bolder. She wanted me to unzip my pants so that she could hold my penis; she wanted to see what it was like. I warned her, "I'll probably come in your hand."

"I want that," she said. "I want to feel it happening."

I hurried to do what she asked, before I came in my pants—just thinking about it. And so it went, for another hour. By the time she was putting her clothes back on, I was already thinking about the next time. How much of this stuff could you do, without actually fucking? I must have been distracted, because on our way back to the door, I knocked something over. It sounded to me like a cannon shot. We froze and listened. For the first time that night, we heard some kind of a noise from Mister Warren's room. We hurried out and down the hall. I thought I heard his door open just as we started down the stairs.

Tuesday was the first day that I relaxed. Marion and I had a date on Saturday, until then I couldn't get into any kind of trouble. I hurried through track practice and then went to look up Freddy. "How was your Thanksgiving?" I asked.

"Great. What have you been up to? You're getting to be a man of mystery around here."

"Oh, the usual stuff. I'm trying to get my Latin grade up. And then there's track."

"Yeah. And?"

"What do you mean *and*?"

"I heard that you got a girl?"

I was sitting on his bed. Freddy sat by the window in what passed for an easy chair, institutional style. It had a simple steel frame with its brown paint wearing off in some places and chipped in others. It had two sturdy black leather cushions: one for the back and one to sit on. I leaned back on my elbows. "I've had a couple of dates. Nothing serious. It's just, you know, an experience."

"Yeah, experience," he said, finally closing his History book and putting it on the windowsill. "Speaking of experience, did I ever tell you about the last time I got laid?"

I sat back up. "Freddy, when you get laid, it will be in the Newark Star Ledger"

"Oh yeah, well when *you* get laid, it's gonna cost you fifty bucks."

I grinned. "Anything new on the Great Homo Hunt?"

Freddy got serious; he leaned forward toward me, as if he was about to tell me a deep dark secret. "I think there were a couple of cops in to see Father Harris yesterday. They spent an hour in his room."

"What makes you think they were cops?"

"My father's a cop. They all wear the same kind of hats and suits. They must get a deal someplace."

"The cops are getting involved?"

"They weren't in there selling life insurance."

I couldn't share my inner thoughts with Freddy; I said, "I thought they'd have found all of them by now."

He sat back in his chair and glanced out the window for a second, then back. "Me too. They sure can't afford to get rid of any more Church students." Then he laughed. "You don't have to worry, unless they've started looking for sex fiends."

I stood up. "You're too much, Freddy, I've got to get back to the books."

Freddy was right; I'd been acting like a loner ever since I met Marion. It just seemed to me that I was already busy, with just about every hour of every day planned out, and even at that, I was behind on my studies. When I added her into my life, especially if you count the time I spent fantasizing over her. I needed to compensate somehow. I also didn't want to give anything away in casual conversations with my buddies. Maybe I'd gone too far; after study period that night I crossed the hall and popped into Charley Duffy's room. "See any good movies while you were home?" I asked.

"Yeah, I saw 'Bataan'. Those fucking Japs; if I ever get over there, I'll kill every one of them. And no prisoners."

"Did they show the 'death march?'"

"Yeah, you wouldn't believe it. Guys got sick, and they bayoneted them right there on the ground."

"Wow. We better win the war, heh?"

"We'll win. I just hope there's time for me to bag a few of those bastards."

"My father says that in ten years we'll be going to Japan on vacations."

"He's crazy. There won't be anything there—just a bunch of bomb craters." Duffy started getting his toilet stuff together. He slung his towel over his shoulder. "You going up?"

"I'll catch up," I said. I wandered down the hall, looking into rooms to see if there was anyone else hanging around that I should socialize with. I passed Mister Fagan's open door. "Steven," he called, "how was your holiday?" He came out to stand in the hallway with me.

"Good," I said. "It was nice to see my friends."

"It's never the same as it was before though, is it?"

I smiled and shook my head. "I guess not."

"You've been busy lately."

I nodded.

"Working on bringing up your Latin, I hope?"

"I'm working on it."

"A Church student can't afford to flunk Latin, you know."

I nodded.

"You'll get it," he said. He gave me a pat on the arm and then turned back into his room. I went back to mine. As I gathered my toilet stuff, it occurred to me that before the end of the week there should be a letter from Irene McNally. Mister Fagan handed out the mail. I should have told her to write on plain white paper. Oh well, I'd tell her next time. What's one pink letter with flowers on it?

Duffy was almost finished when I got to the upstairs washroom. "What did *you* do while you were home?" he asked.

"Not much. Hung around, went to visit my grandmother in Astoria. I went to a party."

"Any interesting girls?"

"Naw. I knew a couple of them in grammar school, real dogs."

"Sure! If one of those *dogs* came over and blew in your ear, you'd be singing a different tune." He packed up to leave.

"You've never seen them," I said.

"I'll see you later." He went out, grinning.

It was getting late; I got busy brushing my teeth. Mister Warren startled me. "Good evening, Steven." He had come in through the open door and was now standing with his hands behind his back, leaning against the door jam. "I was wondering," he asked, "if you've noticed any strangers about, recently?"

I spit out quickly and rinsed my mouth. I dried it off and answered, "I didn't actually see anybody, but Freddy Joyce said that he thought he saw a couple of cops here yesterday." I put the top back onto my toothpaste and put it into my bag along with my brush in its little tube.

"What were they doing? Did, Freddy, say?" He had moved into the room and was standing at the sink next to mine.

"He said that they went in to see Father Harris."

"Were they in uniform?"

"No, but his father's a cop. He says they all dress the same."

He shrugged his shoulders and walked away. "Yes well, who knows what they were. Could be almost anything." He looked at me over his shoulder, and I nodded.

"Thanks, Steven."

I hurried back to my room. After I got into bed and was settling down, I remembered that I wanted to leave the window open a crack. I got up and opened it. Just as I was about to turn away, I glanced down at the basement door, which led out to the rear courtyard—the same door that Marion and I used. Mister Warren was backing out the door, struggling with that same box, the one I'd helped him carry up to his room on Sunday. I watched him wrestle it into his car and then went back to bed. I lay there wondering if he'd stolen something, and it was in that box?

AKE

CHAPTER TEN

Irene's letter came on Friday. Sure enough, it was in a pink envelope—no flowers though. Mister Fagan just handed it to me—no raised eyebrows or anything. I saved it for late that afternoon, after almost all the boarders had gone home for the weekend. I don't know what I expected; it didn't say much, nothing personal, and no picture. She said she was looking for one from me. She said that she was making things for Christmas presents, trying not to use any materials that were needed for the war effort. She said that she enjoyed choir practice at Holy Angels Academy and that there would be a special Christmas concert, open to the public. She ended by telling me that Totsie's, up on the Pike, had been caught selling black market gas. She signed it 'Love', and in a P.S., said she was looking forward to seeing me at Christmas. Okay, I guessed that it would take awhile before she fell madly in love with me.

I brought a present with me to Marion's house on Saturday. It was a charm, a shiny little track shoe that I got for competing in a meet in Jersey City. I gave it to her right away so that she could show it to her mother and grandparents. I wanted her and her family to see that I cared for her. Mostly, I think, I wanted to convince myself that I cared for her. The idea that I only wanted her body repulsed me; I needed for there to be more than that. I was sure that there could be lots more, if I made the effort to look for it.

Marion loved the charm; she went right up to her room to get a chain so that she could wear it around her neck. I stood on the living room rug, being rewarded with warm smiles from her mother and grandparents, while I waited.

She came down and we went out into the cold and headed across the campus to catch a bus on South Orange Avenue. It took about fifteen minutes to get to the movies on Market Street in Newark. Marion wore a black woolen coat. It was tailored, so that you could see the profile of her breasts. I had on my light windbreaker and two sweaters. Duffy had loaned me a nice one for the weekend. We saw 'For Whom the Bell Tolls' with Gary Cooper and Ingrid Bergman. I thought that she had to be the most beautiful woman ever.

On the way back, we got off the bus at the Cricklewood for a soda. There were a couple of seminarians there from the college. I thought that they were looking at me kind of fishy; maybe they knew that I was a Church student, but I didn't know them. So what? Maybe they were just hard up and looking at Marion.

We got back to her house and stood on the porch; I was freezing. It had been a nice date; we talked about all kinds of things, including her father's letters telling about life at sea. We hugged each other and kissed; neither one of us got worked up. "This was nice," I said. "I really feel that I'm getting to know you better."

She clutched the back of my jacket, holding me close. "I had a nice time," she said, "but I still think we should have our special time together."

"Yes," I said, "those times are really special." I couldn't help it; I was getting a hard-on. She was waiting for me to suggest a time. "What, er? When would be a good night?"

"Monday," she said. She kissed me and turned to go inside.

I half trotted back across the campus, hands jammed into my jacket pockets. Monday, I thought. My God! She'll probably want to do it again on Thursday. We're going to get caught; I just knew it. I should have said Wednesday, or Thursday.

I went up to the fourth floor after supper on Monday night to check the closet; I wanted to be sure that it was unlocked and that there weren't any brooms or anything, waiting to be tripped over. I was headed back down the hall when Mister Warren came up the stairs. "Good evening, Steven." He had an odd grin on his face.

"Good evening, sir." I was sure that he hadn't seen me checking out the closet.

When we got to the closet, I was delighted to see that the moon was providing plenty of light. We could see our way clearly to the couch, no need to worry about making too much noise. Marion took off her coat, but she didn't sit down. "Have you ever been to a strip tease?" she whispered.

"No," I answered in a hoarse quiet croak.

She pushed me to sit down on the couch while she stood in the moonlight. I could see her clearly; her lips stood out, shiny black streaks against a face with skin so white in the dim light streaming through the dirty window to my rear. "Make believe that you can hear the music," she said. She took off her cardigan and laid it on top of her coat, then her shoes, then her woolen skirt. Everything was white now except her eyes, her hair and her mouth. She was wearing a full slip; she twirled around in a hip-swinging dance. I had to sit up and pull my pants out from binding up my crotch. She turned her back and lifted her slip, higher and higher until it was off and on top of her skirt. She kept her back to me while she reached behind to undo her bra. I didn't know how much longer I could hold it. She turned and danced up to me, slowly and tantalizingly letting her bra slip off. I reached for her. She backed away, dropping her bra on the pile as she went. Then she came up close again; I wanted to kiss her stomach. She danced back, just a step and slipped her hands under the waistband of her panties. That did it.

I started to come, just as the door burst open. A flashlight shone into the room, landing on Marion's body. The flashlight lingered a moment. I sat, stunned, my mouth open; I was frozen. Marion grabbed her coat and held in front of her; her other clothes spilled to the floor.

"Steven." It was Warren. I don't remember being able to answer.

"Steven. You see this young lady out of the building, and come to see me after school tomorrow." I was grateful when he backed out closing the door.

Marion was half dressed, but having some difficulties. I knelt on the floor to pick up her things and to help her. I wanted so badly too hold her, to tell her that it was all right, that nothing was going to happen to her, to comfort her in some way. Somehow, I helped her to calm down and get her clothes on straight. She rushed out of the basement door without even a kiss. It was a tragedy; I'd never seen anything so beautiful; it shouldn't have ended like that. I didn't care what Warren was going to say or do, I wanted Marion; I needed to hold her.

I fumbled my way through school the next day; Mister Howell and Father Petrocelli both had to call my name twice before I responded, and then, I didn't know what the questions were. After my last class, I went out to track practice, thinking that Mister Warren probably wasn't in his room yet. As I ran up the hill, just alongside the driveway, I glanced up at his window, which had a good view of that part of the campus. I thought that I saw a figure at the window, but when I looked again a second later, it was gone—probably my imagination.

I made up my mind as I was getting dressed after a shower; I would not give him Marion's name, and I would not tell him that I'd decided not to become a priest. When I knocked on his door, my heart was thumping pretty hard; I prayed that I wouldn't blush, and that I could keep my voice from trembling. He opened the door and gestured for me to come in. He pointed to a chair and then sat down in a desk chair, which he swiveled around to face me.

"We won't go over what happened last night," he said. "It's not my purpose to embarrass you any more than necessary."

I sat stiffly in the chair, studying his face for any sign of his intentions. I think he was doing the same; he said nothing but sat there looking me over. Then he said, "I'm sure that you've considered the consequences of this little, er, problem being reported to Father Harris?"

I nodded, trying to look solemn and chastened; maybe he'd decide that I'd already learned my lesson.

He continued, "I doubt that you've considered the long term implications of the situation. Being expelled for something like this could haunt you for the rest of your life. And of course, you'd have to forget about becoming a priest."

"I understand." I wondered how much longer he was going to beat me down.

He continued to study me. "That's why I think that it would be best if this matter went no further."

I held my breath; there had to be more.

He leaned back. "I have my own little secret," he said. "I assume that you'll keep it to yourself?"

I nodded vigorously. "Yes, sir. I certainly will."

"I've been writing a book, Steven. It has to do with all this homosexual business that's been uncovered." He gazed off and then back at me to gauge my reaction.

I just sat there waiting. I had no idea of what the connection could be.

"The fact that I'm writing this book, and the contents of the book have got to be kept a complete secret."

I felt that I needed to say something. "I understand."

"I have to give each chapter to my editor as I complete it, and then to make corrections when he sends it back." He waited for me to nod. Then he said, "Because of the war, we don't feel that we can trust the mail, so the chapters need to be hand carried, back and forth."

I didn't understand why the war would cause him to mistrust the mail, but he sounded as though he knew what he was talking about.

"I need your help, Steven. Can I count on you?"

I had this strange feeling of being totally disconnected from whatever he was talking about and how it might affect me, but I had no choice; I agreed.

"There's not much to it. You go into South Orange about twice a week. Once to cash your check, I believe?"

"Yes, sir. That's right. Also to get my laundry done." I was beginning to relax. It sounded as though he was not going to turn me in, and as long as he didn't want me to rob a bank, or something like that, I guessed that I could do what he wanted.

"I'd like to set it up so that you always go on the same afternoons, and I'd like you to deliver and pick up an envelope. I'll either give you an envelope, or tell you where to find one. You'll go to the South Orange library, go to a certain book, take the envelope that's in the book, and leave the one you bring in its place. Understand?"

"Yes, sir." It seemed simple enough, and I knew that he'd go over it again.

He got up to walk around, pausing to lean over his worktable and gaze out the window. On a wall next to the window, there were some photos that I hadn't noticed before. Apparently Warren was something of a hiker; one was of him by himself, wearing leather shorts and a feathered cap; another showed a group of people similarly dressed. He came back to his chair, sat down and explained how we'd go about the envelope exchange. First, we agreed on the days (Tuesday and Thursday). I'd find an envelope behind the fire hose on the fourth floor and slide the return envelope under his door.

When he finished, and I'd repeated it back, he stood up indicating that it was time to leave. At the door, he handed me a dollar. "It will be worth your while, Steven, but secrecy is paramount." I'd barely left his door when I met Duffy in the hall; he'd seen me leave Warren's room. He put his hand up to his mouth to make the 'ass-kissing' sign. "sweeek, sweeek." I held up the dollar. "He just wants me to wash his car."

I called Marion and told her that Warren was not going to turn me in, and that he hadn't asked me anything about her. "I still can't believe how beautiful you are," I said. Then I asked her to go out again on Saturday night. She agreed, but she didn't sound enthusiastic.

CHAPTER ELEVEN

On Thursday after track, I went to South Orange center, ostensibly to drop off some laundry. The fire hose was right at the top of the stairs on the fourth floor, a dusty old thing folded into a rack. The envelope, a brown paper envelope, was stuck into one of the folds in the back. I slipped it into my laundry bag and headed off. It was probably my imagination, but as I walked down the driveway, I had the feeling that Warren was watching me from his room on the top floor. I turned onto South Orange Avenue and was out of sight; I started to think about this book that Warren was writing. The only reason that he'd want to keep it a deep dark secret was that it was going to be bad for the school, and here I was helping him do it; not that I had any choice.

He said it was going to be about the homosexual scandal, what we kids were calling the 'great homo hunt.' Did he know more about it than we did? Were there details that were known only to certain faculty and priests? I remembered that Duffy had told me about talking to a day hop named Mitchell, and that Mitchell told him that last summer, he'd been hitch-hiking somewhere down on the Jersey shore and that Father Reed had picked him up. Reed was wearing sports clothes, so Mitchell didn't recognize him at first. Reed tried to make him. Ever since then, almost all the boarding students argued about which priests were queer. Freddy said that if they act like tough guys, they're probably queer.

At the library, I found 'Animate Creation', a large book by the Rev. J.G. Wood. I checked to see that no one was watching and then traded the envelopes. Back at the school, I slipped the envelope under Warren's door, and I was finished for the week.

Mister Fagan had a letter for me, a plain white envelope from I. McNally. Good girl! It was a chatty letter, mostly about school. She mentioned her father; the FBI had assigned him to an anti espionage unit. She said that she was worried because that sounded more dangerous than catching bank robbers, and the like. She ended by saying that I was now included in her daily prayers, and might I be interested in attending Midnight Mass with her. There was a P.S. saying that she hoped the other boys hadn't teased me too much about the pink envelope.

I sat at my desk, holding the letter and thinking about what it meant, not the words, but the implications. Here was the most beautiful girl that I'd ever talked to, and it sounded as if she was thinking that she would be my girl. How could this be happening? And how was I supposed to go from Marion, who delighted in putting the intimate parts of her body into my hands, who raised my lust to a flaming frenzy, who made me come before I'd even touched her, to a devote Irish Catholic girl with a movie star's face and those incredible breasts? I knew that I would wind up in love with Irene before New Years, and that it would be a mixed blessing. I planned to go to Confession as soon as I got home for Christmas, and I would stay sin free until . . . Yeah, that was it; I'd stay sin free until the next chance I got. I wondered if Marion would be able to come up with another hide-away somewhere.

On Friday after my last class, I went up to the room, stood in front of my desk, and dropped my books onto it with a loud plop. I leaned on the desk and stared out the window; dayhops came out the basement doors in an almost continuous stream. Their weekends would start when they got home; some of them would study on the bus, and some of them would sit down at a desk as soon as they got home to continue their studies. What a bunch! My weekend had already started, but I still needed to get out for track. I stayed at the window for another minute watching the wind beat leaves and other debris into miniature cyclones around the inside corners of the building. I knew it would be cold out there.

I got into my track stuff and headed down the stairs. The outdoor wooden track was on the far side of the campus; I was tempted to go over the connecting bridge and through the administration building—forbidden territory, unless you were on your way to the chapel. I went out the back and over to the track hut instead. Coach Chamberlain was there. "Doyle, don't bother going to the track today. I want you to get in some distance. Make a loop of the campus, down behind the gym, up to the Archbishop's house, down South Orange Avenue to the corner, and then back around. I'm gonna time you." He took out his pocket watch and made a show of reading the time.

You didn't need to stand very close to Chamberlain to get a good whiff of the whiskey that he fortified himself with every afternoon. He stood around outside the hut, or on the track, talking to each of us. He rarely addressed us as a group. On this day, his overcoat collar was turned up, his old fedora pulled down, and his hands were in his pockets. He called to those still in the hut. "Harry, don't dawdle, you'll catch cold." Peter Flynn had just come out and was starting to stretch; I was doing the same. "Forget that, you two, get moving. It's too cold."

"Okay," I said, "we're starting."

He nodded and took out his watch again.

Peter was grinning from ear to ear as we set off. "Do you think he can read the time?"

"He can, but he won't remember what it was," I said.

We often joked like this, all of us on the track team, but we never mentioned his drinking to anyone else. We knew that the priests had to know about it, and that someday they'd probably fire him. We wanted to protect him as long as we could. We felt the warmth of the man; he knew us each by name and would greet us anywhere. He cared for us, and it came through in his kindly words and concern. Maybe that's why his teams were so good. We ran hard that day; it didn't matter that he'd forget the time.

After I showered, I went to look up Freddy; he was staying for the weekend because he'd flunked some test and had to study for a makeup. Freddy was a fun guy to hang around with, but he did have a knack for getting into trouble, and I don't think that the teachers and proctors liked him very much. No matter what he was wearing, he managed to look a little bit sloppy. The top button on his shirt was never done; his tie was always down and loose, and he always had some kind of junk stuffed into the pockets of his sport jackets. It didn't help that he was flabby, and that his shoes were never shined. But I liked him; he was never dull.

I met Freddy coming down the hall. "Hey, Steve," he says to me as we converged on his room, "I see your buddy, George Patton is in big trouble for slapping a soldier."

"So?" I said. "The guy probably deserved it." I was a big fan of George Patton.

"Doesn't look good," Freddy said, as he opened his door

and we went in. "The guy was in a hospital with battle fatigue. He'd been in combat for four months."

"I'll pray for both of them," I said. "What do you want to do tonight?"

Freddy shrugged. "I don't care."

"Let's go to the CYO dance in East Orange."

"Wowee! You *are* getting to be a nooky hound."

We left at seven; it would take two short bus rides to get to East Orange. There was plenty of room on the first bus; we sat in the back, two buddies out on the town. It was a time for serious conversation.

"What do you think of Stanton getting the ax?" Freddy asked.

"Huh?" I had thought that Stanton, a teacher who had a room in our building and who sometimes filled in as a proctor, was out sick.

"The great homo hunt finds another pervert."

"He's queer?" I said.

"Come on, Doyle, you knew."

I shrugged. "I wasn't sure," I said. I looked out the window; I didn't want to talk any more just then. I had that same sick feeling in my stomach. I had been hoping, praying that they were finished, that they'd found out all they needed to know, and that all the homos had been expelled or fired. I didn't know of any that were left. Maybe they already knew about me and had decided to let it pass. Maybe they were still digging and would uncover my shame. Maybe they'd come back and deal with me after they purged all the homos.

Freddy was poking me in the ribs. "What about Warren?"

"Wha..? What about him?"

"Is he queer?"

"I don't think so."

"You should know."

"*Freddy,* I hardly ever talk to the guy."

"Yes but, *Steven,* you're the *only* one *he* talks to."

We got up to stand by the door and get off at the next stop. Freddy went on. "You don't want to go down with the ship. No pun intended."

Getting off the bus, I said, "Freddy, stop being such a jerk."

We went up the steps of the parish hall, paid our dimes, got our hands stamped with purple ink, and went inside. A four-piece band, composed of kids who looked even younger than we were, was tuning up on stage. The center of the room was left open for dancing, but kids were milling around on all sides. I spotted a couple of guys in uniform; they'd get the best girls. It didn't seem fair. The girls all wore a type of uniform themselves: sweaters, pleated skirts, bobby socks, and saddle shoes. I was wearing my new maroon corduroy jacket. I kept it buttoned because my pants were too big and were bunched up around my waist. Freddy made a quick tour of the room to check out the girls. "There are some real dolls here," he reported. I had been looking around for a girl who didn't look like she'd be real popular, a little fat and not too short. I hoped that the band would start with a slow number. They didn't. I had real misgivings about putting my jitterbugging on display after only that one lesson with Marion.

By the time they played a slow one, I'd found my fat girl. Her name was Claire. I didn't hold her close but her breasts kept bumping into me anyway. It didn't matter; I was wearing a tight jock underneath my underwear. After two slow dances and two fast ones, I left Claire and walked around to find Freddy. He'd been dancing with a good-looking girl named Alice who introduced me to her friend Lucia, a big improvement over Claire.

We danced, talked, bought Cokes, and then had to leave early to get back to school. Freddy took Alice's telephone number, and I took Lucia's. Freddy was excited; on the way back to the bus, he said, "Did you see how she was putting it to me right there on the dance floor?" I mumbled some kind of reply. "Man," he said, "I had a hard-on like a brick. She kept rubbing up against it. She liked it. I could tell."

"I hope that you're not too uncomfortable," I said.

"Hah. I'm used to it. Only amateurs come in their pants."

Saturday dragged, and that was just fine with me. I hadn't figured out how to play it with Marion. I really did like her, but I knew that I'd never be in love with her; all that I could ever think about was her body, and now we had no place to go for that. I was sure that she wanted more and more from me, and I couldn't be more willing; I even planned to go into Newark to try to buy some condoms. If only I could figure out a way not to blush. I worried that I would not be able to keep her interested.

Our date was okay, better than I expected. Marion was chatty and very passionate when we kissed goodnight. She surprised me when she said that her mother wanted me to come to dinner on Sunday afternoon. Then she said that her father was home for a short leave and wanted to meet me. What did that mean?

I was tempted to talk with Freddy about my dinner invitation, but I figured he'd just say things that would wind up making me more nervous; so I didn't.

It rained on Sunday. I was pretty wet and had to take off my soggy shoes when I got to Marion's house. One of my socks had a hole in it; I'd forgotten about that. And I didn't have anything to bring; nobody seemed to notice that or my sock.

Mister Fletcher was very nice; his questions were kindly ones. I didn't say anything about being a Church student, but I did tell him about my family and that I was at the Prep on a special loan program. I didn't say anything about my father, either. I asked him about the Merchant Marine; he was an executive officer on a cargo ship. He sailed in convoys to England and to Africa. I knew that the Merchant Marine had really gotten clobbered in the first eighteen months of the war, and that it was still extremely dangerous.

We sat in the living room, which was the front room of the house. I sat on the couch, about two feet away from Marion, facing the front windows. Her grandparents sat in two chairs to our left, and Mister Fletcher sat in an easy chair to my right front, just alongside the window. There was a small chair to my right that Mrs. Fletcher sat in when she wasn't busy in the kitchen. I asked Mister Fletcher a question. "Have you ever been torpedoed?"

He smiled and glanced over at his wife who sat stiffly with her hands clasped on her lap. "I'm really not at liberty to discuss that, Steve, but the submarine threat has subsided by quite a bit." He nodded to his wife. "The FBI tells us that they've got almost all the spies rounded up, the ones that were sending out information for the wolf packs."

"How would they know?" It immediately flashed through my mind that if I ever met Irene's dad, I could ask *him*.

He laughed. "I'm not sure, but I suspect that they monitor the airwaves, and if they don't find much, and the subs don't find us, well . . . "

I nodded. Marion reached for my hand. "We don't like to talk about it," she said.

I looked over to her mother. "I'm sorry," I said. "I'm very sorry." I felt myself starting to blush. She got up and came over to put a hand on my shoulder. "It's nothing to apologize for, Steven. We're just a little superstitious."

After dinner, which was great, Marion asked if I'd like to go down to the basement and play pool. "Sure, you can give me a lesson," I said. Marion gave me a glare. We went downstairs and she uncovered the pool table. She racked up the balls and then handed me a cue. I picked a piece of chalk off the shelf and started to chalk the tip. She came up against my side, circled her arm around my waist, and pressed her hand on my stomach, just below my belt. "What kind of lesson did you have in mind?" she asked.

Bang, instant hard-on, and her father was no more than two seconds away. We played pool, or at least pretended to. Marion kept grinning at me. I knew that she could see it. There were some little hugs and kisses in between shots. When it was time to leave, she went with me to the bottom of the stairs. She put one arm around me and put her other hand down on my crotch for two hard rubs. "You'll be all right," she said. I wasn't. I promised to call her.

It had stopped raining, but my shoes were still wet; they were cold too. On my walk back across the campus, I tried to distract myself with a sex fantasy featuring Marion with all her clothes off, and me having finally acquired a condom. I still couldn't wait until I got to my room to take my shoes off. As I got to the third floor, I heard the usual yelling back and forth; almost all the boarders were back from their weekends. "Hey, Vinny." It was Duffy's voice. "I hear the Italians are gonna invade Rome." All the Italian kids took a ribbing over Mussolini, and all those Italians who surrendered in North Africa. Now that they'd switched sides, and were fighting for the Allies, there was a whole new supply of jokes. Vinny gave as good as he got. "Yeah, Duffy, I hope the Irish sober up long enough to get their potatoes planted this year." I went straight to my room, put on my other shoes and went down to wait on tables.

I got back to my room ten minutes before study period started. I used the time to write a thank-you note to Mrs. Fletcher. I added that I would pray for Mister Fletcher's safe return from his voyages. I licked the bitter, dry glue, and as I sealed the envelope, I wondered if it was a good idea for me to be praying for somebody like that. Maybe God would kill him, just to teach me a lesson. No, I decided, maybe God actually listened harder to prayers from sinners. The bell rang for the start of study period; I found a stamp, stuck onto the envelope, and then opened my Latin book. Why did I always feel as if my head was being squeezed by some monster when I worked on this stuff? After a half-hour, I sat back to stretch and take a deep breath; I glanced at the envelope addressed to Marion's mom. My mind began to wander. I wondered if I could talk Marion into going back to the fourth floor; Warren wasn't in any position to rat on us, but what could I tell her that would convince her?

CHAPTER TWELVE

Father Petrocelli had been calling on me more frequently during the last month; I assumed that it was to bring home the gravity of my situation: a Church student barely scraping by in Latin. "Steven, please give us your Latin translation of the first paragraph of last night's homework." I went through the motions of flipping pages in my notebook while sliding slowly to the edge of my seat. I knew that one of his standard jokes was on its way. "Rise and shine, Steven," there was a brief pause, "Rise anyway." He had another old chestnut that he'd use if I were just a bit slower. "Don't sit there letting us think that you're a dolt." pause, "Stand up and remove all doubt." These jokes and others, were standard fare in every class. They were not aimed at me, or anyone in particular, but were intended to lighten things up.

Petrocelli always wore a cassock and liked to sit on the front of the teacher's desk with his legs dangling, sometimes kicking the hollow panel of the desk for a sound-effect exclamation point. He was about five foot eight, rotund and had the cheerful face of a monk, behind steel rimmed glasses.

I began my recitation; he wrote it on the board—having no difficulty in keeping up with my halting Latin. At the end, he made a big dash with the chalk and turned. "Domenico, what do you think?" Domenico looked up and said that he had it somewhat different. Of course he would; the bastard spoke Italian at home and studied ten hours a night. He aced every test. Petrocelli said, "Yes, but it's not bad, Steven. You need to work on your irregular verbs." Then he asked, "Who would like to give us the next paragraph? Don't be shy. Here's your opportunity: flunk now and avoid the rush in June."

A young student, probably a freshman, appeared at the door, knocked and came in to hand Petrocelli a note. Petrocelli, who was perched on the front of the desk again, looked at the note, dismissed the student, and called my name. "Father Harris wants to see you in his room." He crumpled the note. I picked up my books and headed for the door, all kinds of horrible possibilities streaming through my head: there'd been a death in my family; the school was going to bounce me because of my Latin; they knew about Marion. The most frightening possibility was that I was now going to be interrogated for the 'great homo hunt.'

I knew the routine from the reports of earlier victims. Father Harris, as headmaster, had a small suite. The first room was a sitting room, nicely furnished with big windows on the far wall facing the door. There would be three priests; two sitting on the couch with the windows to their backs and the coffee table in front of their knees. Father Harris would sit in a large, light green, winged back chair to the right side. One of the priests, probably Father Sullivan, would stand, hand me a bible, and ask me to put my hand on it and swear to tell the truth. How could I? Would they press me for the intimate details? What did they care, anyway? They'd already uncovered Shoals and dismissed him last year. Maybe they got him to tell everything before he left, and they were just getting around to dealing with me. For all these months they'd known; every time they looked at me they knew.

Father Harris's room was on the third floor; his door was in the corner in between Mr. Fagan's, which was on the hall leading to my room and Mr. Stanton's, which was on the main corridor. It was dark in that corner, and the door was painted black. I stood in front of that door for a full minute, thinking, in a hopeless kind of way, that some kind of miracle might intervene. I submitted myself with a light knock on the door.

Father Harris opened the door and motioned for me to come in. He was smiling; he seemed genuinely glad to see me. As soon as he got out of the way, I shot a look at the couch—no priests. Instead, there were two men in suits, the cops! My God, I thought, my father's done something, or maybe it's just one of my crazy uncles.

"Steven, these gentlemen are from the FBI: Mr. Taylor and Mr. Lynch."

They nodded; obviously, they already knew my name. Harris pointed to a chair in front of the couch. There was a small side table next to it. "Those are for you, Steven." There were cookies and milk on the table. I sat down, had a small bite of one cookie, a sip of milk, and waited. These guys weren't here for anything to do with Marion, or homos.

Taylor spoke, "Steve, we understand that you've had some contacts with Mr. Warren. Is that right?"

I didn't know what to say. I could say 'yes' to that question, but what about the next one? What happens when Warren squeals on *me*? I guess I looked pretty stunned because Father

Harris got up and asked me to step into the next room. He closed the door behind us. "Steven, these men need your help in a very serious situation. It's not about the girl; we know about her, and those things are sins of the flesh. We are all sinners, and God forgives us these things. Put it out of your mind; help these men, and everything will be fine."

I nodded, "Thank you, Father." We went back inside. "Yes," I said, "that's right."

"Okay, Steve," Lynch spoke, "you're doing some kind of errands for Warren?"

"Yes."

"Would you—and just take your time please—tell us the details of what you're doing? And tell us what he told you about the reasons."

I knew it! The homo business was going to get into it no matter what I did. I decided not to fool around with the FBI. I set out to tell them everything. The Marion part I skimmed over, never saying what I'd done, but only that Warren promised not to snitch if I helped him.

"So, he told you that these were chapters for a book?" Taylor asked.

"Yes, sir."

"And the reason it had to be kept secret is that it was about the recent homosexual incidents here at the school?"

I glanced at Father Harris. The three men all exchanged glances and nods; they had obviously discussed the homo business and had an understanding.

"Yes, sir," I said. "That's right."

"Okay, Steve," Lynch took over, "we're going to tell you something, but first we've got to swear you to secrecy."

I nodded, waiting for the bible to come out.

"This is so secret, you can't even tell it in Confession. Understand?"

I looked at Father Harris. Could that be right? Father Harris nodded, "It's all right, Steven."

I turned back to Lynch. "Yes, sir."

He looked to Taylor and then back to me. "Steve, Warren is a German spy."

I know that my mouth must have dropped open at that point. Taylor sat leaning forward with his hands folded in front of him. He waited for a few seconds. "You can walk out that door right now, Steve, and just keep your mouth shut. Or, you can stay and work with us. You should know that it can be extremely dangerous, and that we'll have to get your parents permission if you say 'yes'."

A German spy! A German spy! It was banging around in my head. I don't know how long it took me to answer. "My parents are good Americans, sir, and I'm willing to die for my country."

The two FBI guys leaned back, and all three men nodded to each other.

"We won't let it come to that, Steve," Lynch said. Taylor picked up the phone, sitting on a side table between him and Father Harris; he spoke briefly to somebody. After he hung up, he addressed me. "Here's what we want you to do." He and Taylor alternated in explaining what they wanted. It was Tuesday, so I would pick up Warren's envelope as expected. Instead of going straight to the library, I would stop at the Post Office. There would be a newspaper sitting on a table near the far end; I would find another envelope in the newspaper; I was to switch the envelopes and then go to the library with the new envelope. "When you leave, there will be a black Plymouth sedan with New York plates waiting at the corner. Get in the back," Taylor said. "Yeah, and we'll be watching you the whole way," Lynch added.

They had me repeat the whole thing back to them, and then I got up to leave. Father Harris accompanied me to the door. "Go back to your last class as if nothing had happened, Steven. If anyone asks, tell them that it was about your problems with Latin. And, Steven, my prayers will be with you every step of the way. God bless you." He handed me a note to get back into class.

My last class was in Geometry, a favorite subject, I was good at it; which was too bad because I didn't need to pay close attention; I could start to worry instead.

I didn't have enough laundry to bother with, so I went empty handed up to the fourth floor and fished behind the fire hose for the envelope. It wasn't there. "Steven!" It was an urgent loud whisper from Warren who was standing in the doorway to the washroom. He jerked his head for me to come to him. I went quickly and he pulled me inside. "There's been a change in plans." He handed me the envelope. He looked a little disheveled, and he kept blinking as he spoke. Something was bugging him; I felt a slight twinge of pity. "You don't go to the library with this. You go to the South Orange train station. Sit on the bench next to the Railway Express office, on the Newark bound side. A man will sit next to you; he'll open a newspaper: The New York Times. He'll ask for the envelope. You give it to him, and that's it. Okay?" He went over it again, and then watched me put the envelope in my pocket. He almost pushed me out into the corridor. The whole time, I hadn't said a single word.

I headed toward the other stairway, the one near the Administration Building. He followed me to the top of the stairs. "I'm going to cut through," I said, "It's cold outside." He nodded, and I saw him head back to his room as I went down. I knew that he'd be looking for me on the driveway in two minutes. I thought about racing along the third floor corridor, to Father Harris's room, to tell him of the change, but Warren might not have gone to his room. Maybe, he'd be waiting on the other stairwell. The FBI said that they'd be watching, but where? Would they still want me to go ahead? Should I go to the Post Office? The envelope was in my inside breast pocket; it was my 'Red Badge of Courage.' I could feel it, like some kind of glowing presence. I was a soldier now; it was up to me to do my duty; I had to show up on the driveway for Warren to see. I had to carry out my mission.

On the second floor, I crossed the bridge, went through the middle building and into the Administration Building. I walked along the second floor where the priests lived. Normally, I'd be sneaking through, or going down to the first floor; this time I wanted to be caught, to run into a priest, one that I knew. Father Petrocelli! I was passing his room. I banged on his door. When he opened it, he pulled his head back in surprise. I could read his mind; how could a borderline Latin student, a Church student no less, have the temerity to bang on his door like that?

I jumbled it out. "Father, please. I know this is crazy. Please, please tell Father Harris that there's been a change, and that I'm going to South Orange train station."

He just stood there staring at me.

"Please, Father, please." I ran off down the hall.

"Steven!" he called after me. I kept going.

I walked down the driveway, outside the trees, to be sure that Warren could see me. At the end of the driveway on South Orange Avenue, I turned left glancing around to see if I could spot anyone following me. I didn't see anyone; maybe they were really good at this sort of thing, but maybe they were waiting near the library. I tried to walk at my normal pace, but I couldn't tell if I was going too fast, or too slow. What if I met Marion? Should I stop and act normal, or keep pushing on?

How did Warren know to change my instructions? Why was he so nervous? Did he have a contact who knew about the FBI? Was that person watching me?

I thought about the war, about the GIs dying overseas, about the men who threw themselves onto hand grenades to save their buddies. I thought about Marion's dad and all those submarine wolf packs waiting to intercept his convoy and send his ship to the bottom while he struggled for a few minutes in the icy cold waters of the North Atlantic, doomed to die because if a ship stopped, it too would be torpedoed. It was my turn now; I had to come through. If I died and nobody ever knew, that's how it would be. Maybe someday, Irene's dad would casually mention this kid at Seton Hall Prep who went out to do his duty and gave up his life for his country. "Some kid named Doyle," he'd say, and Irene would go off to her room to hold my picture and quietly sob for hours.

I was already there; it seemed too short. I walked up the steps and into the Post Office; surely, somebody from the FBI was watching me by now. I tried to act casual, as if I'd come in to get some stamps, or to read the wanted posters. Only a few people were around, and they all seemed to have some specific business in hand. There, at one end of the large, marble floored room, was the table and the newspaper. I just casually strolled up; it's not every day that you find a free newspaper in the Post Office. Looking it over, I very carefully switched the envelopes. Nobody took notice.

I skittered down the steps, confident that somebody had to be watching me at that point, and headed back toward South Orange Avenue and the train station, not the library. It did occur to me that everything had been arranged on short notice, and maybe they only had enough time to get somebody to the library to watch for me. Well, that would be their fault, I'd just complete the mission and go back to school.

I passed Wilson's soda fountain; girls were coming and going, but I didn't see anyone I knew. Marion might have been inside—ships passing in the night. At the bottom of the hill, I walked up the stairs to the train platform and looked around. There was nobody in sight; it looked like there was plenty of time before I had to do anything; I read the train schedule. In twenty minutes, there would be a train for Newark. It was cold so I jumped up and down a bit and then jogged up and down the platform. I found myself at the bench next to the Railway Express office; I sat down, pulled up my collar and waited; nothing happened. There was nobody on either side of the tracks. Finally, I saw somebody, a man, come onto the platform. He stayed down the other end. I looked at the clock; the train was due in five minutes. Some other people came onto the platform: some women with shopping bags, two mothers with small children, and then a couple of business men—maybe the FBI, at last.

The man from the other end of the platform walked in my direction; he wore a dark colored, thick woolen overcoat and a gray fedora which was pulled down as if to guard against the cold. He kept looking at his watch and then at the two business men. When he got close, he came over and sat down. He had a New York Times, but he did not open it or say anything. The two business men seemed to have moved further away. I thought that I could hear the train coming. Nothing was happening; nobody was talking; nobody looked like they were getting ready to get on the train. It was like a movie that had just stopped. I was sitting in the middle of a still picture of a train station.

Now I could feel the faint vibrations of the train in my feet; I was sure that I could hear it. The man next to me stirred; he moved his newspaper to a different position on his lap. He lifted part of it and spoke. "You get on the train and stay right in front of me."

I started to turn, to say something. He lowered his eyes. I glanced down to see the gun in his lap, inside the fold of The New York Times. Now the platform was throbbing; the train in the station. I looked for the business men—nowhere. The man with the gun nudged me to get up and onto the train.

The train was not too crowded; not many people were going into the city at that time of day. We got on at the front of a car, and I went down the aisle looking for a familiar face. "Sit here," the man said. I sat down and he took the seat immediately behind me. "Take it," he said. His voice was right behind my ear, low and gruff. I thought I detected the hint of an accent, but it could have been my imagination. A ticket appeared at my elbow. I took it; I wanted to turn around, to get a good look at his face. Something told me that I should keep my eyes straight ahead. I held the ticket like a flower in my lap.

So far, he hadn't mentioned the envelope. Did he know that it wasn't the original, or was he thinking he'd have me leave it somewhere, or give it to someone else? The train stopped in Harrison; a few people got off, and about six people got on. They all looked like workers and housewives. Where the hell was the FBI? The conductor came through, taking tickets. I stared into his eyes as I handed him my ticket; even holding onto it a little so that he had to pull. He didn't even look at me. He was just some sixty year old guy plodding away until retirement, every inch a typical looking conductor.

Suppose the FBI didn't know anything about what was happening? Maybe Father Petrocelli hadn't told anybody about the change, and maybe, the FBI had people in the wrong places. What did this guy want with me? Where was he taking me?

Some girls came into the car—school girls, my own age. There were five of them, each wearing a short winter jacket, pleated skirt, bobby socks, and a colorful babushka. Instead of using a book bag, they carried their books in the crook of one arm. They were giggling and laughing as the train rocked them from side to side, and they had to grab onto seat backs, and sometimes people, as they came down the aisle. I sat just past the middle of the car. When the first girl spotted me, she said something back over her shoulder to the next one, and the word was passed along. I could tell that I was in for a hard time. I hated it when girls did this to me; it was some kind of sport to them, and they would all scream and laugh when I turned fire-engine red.

I'd been scared all afternoon; now it was worse. I could feel my heart pounding and the sweat starting to flow; I took deep breaths. What would the guy with the gun do? Suppose these girls wouldn't quit? Suppose they just kept it up? Would he panic and shoot me?

The first girl stopped. "Look what I found." They crowded around. "We should take him home," another said. At other times when girls had done this to me, I kept my eyes on the ground. This time I looked up, thinking that I could silently plead with them to stop. "Oow. Look at those baby blue *eyes*," one said. At that point the situation was getting so crazy, I started to laugh. It wasn't exactly a laugh; more like a rattling in my throat. "He's so cute. Wouldn't you like to find him under your tree at Christmas?"

The gruff voice spoke into my ear. "Tell your friends to go away." This time, I was sure that there was an accent. I half-turned to explain: "They won't do it." In that instant, I thought that I should get up and go with the girls. What could he do? But, he might be desperate, I thought.

The man with the gun spoke again. "Girls, his mother just passed away. He's going home to the funeral." They all looked horrified. They filed past, each one touching my shoulder and saying, "I'm sorry."

I was relieved; I didn't have to make a decision; nothing would happen until we got off the train. Where would that be? I never looked at my ticket, but the last stop was the ferry dock in Jersey City where you got on the ferry for New York. Maybe we were going into New York City. Maybe I was going into the Hudson River.

I moved my eyes to check out my seat companion, an old woman with gnarled hands folded on her lap, and a cloth shopping bag at her feet. She wore a shabby looking woolen coat and a gray knit woolen hat. She was staring absently straight ahead at the back of the seat in front of her. Her head moved in slight small nods, and her lips moved as if in silent prayer. Clearly, she could be of no help to me. I wondered what she could be thinking about. I've heard that old people day dream about their pasts. Was she reviewing her long life? Thinking about a husband who died years ago?

That's what I'd like to do someday: think about my youth when I got involved with German spies and lived to tell about it. We were coming into Jersey City. It was getting dark and the bleak old buildings, which seem to line the tracks in all old cities—the backwash of earlier prosperity—made me feel that everything was ending. The train was slowing to a crawl; people were putting on overcoats and taking packages from the overhead rack. I waited. The train stopped; everyone was active; the old woman next to me stirred and turned the upper half of her body in my direction. She had her hand on her bag. I thought that I could jump up and run like hell into the crowd.

I slid to the outside of my seat. A hand grabbed my shoulder. "Just let her out." I turned my legs to the outside.

The old woman got up and slipped past, nodding and giving me a small smile. The wrinkles on her face were deeper and sharper than I'd ever seen before; she looked like the subject of one of those stark pictures taken during the depression.

"Stand up." I did, and immediately felt him grab the back of my jacket, just at the small of my back. "Just move as I tell you."

We got off the train, looking like a couple of jerks on the stairs. Then came the walk along the platform toward the station and the ferryboats. Something had to happen soon. In a few minutes he could be clunking me over the head and dropping me into the river, or he could have me in a car headed for a hide out. I had to do something, and I had to pee something fierce.

We got to the end of the platform—he kept pushing me—toward the ferryboats. "I gotta pee," I said.

"You can go on the boat."

"They're not letting people on yet."

"You're going to wait."

"I can't. I can't. I'm gonna pee in my pants. It's going to go all over. It's going to be a lot." I felt the pressure on my back ease.

He moved me to the side, away from the streams of people headed for trains or the ferry. For the first time, I was face to face with my captor, my very own German spy. He was the same height, maybe even a little shorter than I am. He cocked his head so that the brim of his cap was just above his eyes, and I looked into his face. His eyes were a pale gray, and the edges of his eyelids were reddened from lack of sleep, or irritation. His face was thin; his lips were thin, and I noticed that his bottom teeth crowded against each other and formed a staggered, crooked row. He seemed to have to work hard to pronounce his words. "We go to the toilet. I watch you. No funny business. You better go!"

All of a sudden, I worried about it. How could I pee with him watching me; ready to shoot me if I didn't go. We went inside. It was a stinky place with gum wrappers stuck to the floor by many wet feet. I went up to a urinal. He stood behind; he wasn't actually going to watch me pee. I stood there; it took a while just to start. Men came and went; stalls opened and closed. I wondered how long I could stand there, enjoying my last moments. Maybe when I turned around he'd be gone!

"Enough," the voice said. I turned around, zipped up, and started for the sinks. His hand on the back of my jacket, jerked me back and pointed me toward the door. We came to the outside, back to the rushing of people. I slowed up, waiting for him to push me, or turn me. Nothing. I stopped; I waited, still nothing. I wavered; should I run? Should I look back?

Passers by slowed to stare at me, to stare at something behind me. I turned. He was gone! I caught a glimpse of three men rushing someone off to the side. All I could see of him was that dark overcoat and his shoes.

CHAPTER THIRTEEN

"Steven! Steven!" Father Harris was standing on the other side. He towered over the people streaming between us. His arms were open for me to come. I ran to him and crashed up against him. He squeezed me. "God listened to our prayers today, Steven."

Mister Lynch was standing just behind him. He came up and we started to move off. "Sorry, we weren't able to give you any signals, Steve. That was a great idea you had, getting him off to the side by going to the bathroom." He patted me on the back.

"We're going back to the Prep now, Steven," Father Harris said. "But you won't be staying there; our friends from the FBI want to be sure that everything is safe before you come back."

A thousand questions popped into my mind; I guess that I must have looked worried.

"Don't worry," Harris said, "we'll have you home for Christmas. In the meantime you'll be staying at Our Lady of Hope Retreat House, as a guest of the good sisters."

He gazed down at me, almost beaming. Was he serious? Were they really going to stick me into a convent?

"One of the sisters, Sister Josephine, is a well known Latin scholar. She's promised to tutor you."

He wasn't kidding.

"Of course, we'll send your other school work along as well, so that you don't fall behind. It should be an interesting experience for you, Steven."

"Yes, Father."

Mister Lynch was laughing; I think he was reading my mind. We got to the car, a black Plymouth with New York plates, and drove to the Prep. Everyone was at supper, and I was starving, but Mister Lynch said that we'd eat on the way. Father Harris took my hands and said good bye. "I'll be in frequent touch with the sisters to be sure that you're all right." I packed practically everything I owned into the same old suitcase with the broken handle and my laundry bag, and Mister Lynch helped me carry them to the car.

On the way down the driveway, Lynch glanced over at me and grinned, "I bet when you show up, they're gonna lock up all the young ones."

"The young nuns?"

"Yeah, Steve. It's going to be a rough ten days. You got a girl at home?"

Maybe he didn't know that I was a Church student. Maybe he knew, but he also knew about Marion. God! Who didn't know about Marion? "I know a couple," I said.

We ate at a diner and got to the retreat house after nine. The Mother Superior met me. She didn't greet me; she met me, looking me over like some kind of common criminal. Another nun showed me to my room. She explained to me that Mass was at six, and that I was expected for breakfast in the kitchen at seven. After that, I'd be told when I could use the library and other facilities. I was not to wander about. A bell would wake me at five-thirty.

When she finished, she said that her name was Sister Saint George. She smiled at me—a warm and friendly smile. She was an old woman; a bit over weight and slightly bent, but her face, held firm in the starched white grasp of her habit, was sparkly and hinted at a bit of mischief. "I'll see that you get enough to eat," she said.

She closed the door, leaving me to sit on the bed and take in my surroundings. I was only half interested; I went to the window. I could make out the dim images of some other buildings and some large trees, but that was all. I went back to sit on the bed; it was hard, but I probably wouldn't be able to sleep anyway. Five-thirty! It was going to be one of those nights when the bell that wakes you, is the only thing that convinces you that you slept at all.

I got up again and started to put my things away in the small dresser and tiny closet. I put my books on the table that served as a desk, got undressed and went into the bathroom. The bathroom was almost as big as my room, all white tile and old-fashioned. There was a huge tube, one of those with ball and claw feet. The most interesting thing was the show head, suspended over the business end of the tub; it looked like the spout of an oversized watering can, a pie plate with holes punched in it.

I pulled down the covers and took a last look around—all white walls with a crucifix over the bed and a holy water fount by the door. And that was it. At that moment, I sensed that my life would never be the same, and that circumstances, more than plans, rule our lives.

I wrote to Marion telling her that I'd been sent away for special studies, and that I would look her up as soon as I got back to school. My exile lasted for ten very long days. Sister Josephine tutored me in Latin every day. I think that she regarded our sessions as some kind of penance, which she offered up for the greater honor and glory of God. My other schoolwork arrived every two or three days, in a nicely organized package. I felt that I was making real progress—even in Latin. There were no distractions! When I thought about girls, I was able to contain my fantasies because of the church-like environment that pervaded every nook and cranny of that place. Mother Superior saw to it that I had no idle time and that I was rarely out of some older nun's oversight. She seemed to be afraid that, if left to my own devices, I'd find some way to contaminate the whole place and she'd have to get a bishop to come and sprinkle holy-water everywhere I'd been.

Christmas vacation brought my stay at Our Lady of Hope to an end, and I headed for Coytesville, itching to see Irene. In Nunguesses, I boarded the small blue bus that ran from there to Englewood Cliffs, and then back through Coytesville on Route 9W. I don't know why they ran that bus; it was always almost empty. I took a window seat near the back on the right hand side and stared out the window thinking about what I'd been through and trying to see some connection to the future. Familiar scenery didn't even register until we passed through Fort Lee and got on the road along the Palisades. There were nothing but woods on my side; we passed Carpenter's Pond where I used to ice-skate, and paths were I rode my bike. We were getting close now. What would I find at home?

I hadn't bought any presents; I wouldn't have even if I hadn't been at the convent. It would be better to give my Christmas money to my mother; we could decide together how to spend it. Would she be pregnant, as I suspected at Thanksgiving? And my sisters? Would they have been drawn into the unhappiness by now? Would they ask *me* to explain? Expect me to do something?

I wished the driver a Merry Christmas and got off the bus. As I went down the hill and passed Jilly's vegetable store, someone called, "Steve, hey, Stevey."

It was Jilly, coming out of the store. Oh God, I thought, he's not going to tell me that our tab is too high and that I should talk to my mother.

He grabbed something on the way out and handed it to me. It was a bag of walnuts. "Here, Stevey, for Christmas. Tell your mother. Merry Christmas." He went back inside.

I said, "Merry Christmas." I think he heard me. I looked at the bag; should I try to give it back? Taking it was a fraud. He only gave it to me because he thought I was going to be a priest. Should I make an announcement right now and give back the nuts? I walked down the hill.

She was pregnant. I didn't say anything. All she said was, "Maybe this time you'll get a little brother." I didn't tell her that it was too late. That I'd be an old man by the time the kid got to be any fun.

She had some bruises on her face. There were probably more on her arms, covered over with a long-sleeved sweater. We didn't talk about that either.

I wanted to cheer her up. "I didn't buy any presents, Mom. I have a little money. Maybe you and I can decide on what to get?"

She smiled and put her hand out to touch my shoulder. "Do you think you could get us some milk? We have no milk."

I nodded, put on my coat and slogged back up the hill into town. It wouldn't just be milk; I'd have to buy some other things as well. To hell with Christmas. By the time I got to town, I was boiling. I not only didn't wish anybody a Merry Christmas, I was barely civil. I just wanted to buy the stuff, dump it at the house, and go to see Irene. Too bad I couldn't stay at her house.

On the way home, I tried to calm down, but I couldn't. I remembered how I used get a kick out of the jokes that my father made out of being so poor. About the bill collectors hiding in the bushes; about how we'd have to change our names and move to Alaska. Then I remembered the times that the electricity got turned off, and when there was no coal for the furnace, and when I had to stay with an aunt, "Just until your father gets back on his feet," my mother would say. And the car, which his mother had given to him, and how that just disappeared one day. "He owes too much money. They were coming after him," my mother said. And the time I couldn't go to my Nana's funeral because I couldn't be seen in the best clothes that I owned. It wasn't funny. It was stupid. Stupid!

I didn't even take off my coat. I put the groceries away, mumbled something to my mother and went off to see Irene. During that vacation, I saw her almost every day. She had an unbelievable ability to indulge in passionate necking, complete with panting, squirming and moaning, and then to crack down with an iron will just when I was almost there. We went to Midnight Mass, followed by a chaste kiss, but we really got into it on New Year's Eve. But that's not what I remember most about that night.

Some lights were on in the kitchen when I got home. I hadn't expected anybody to be up, now I had to worry about lipstick stains on my face or collar. There was some noise coming from the kitchen, so being as quiet as possible, I let myself in the front door. One of my sisters had the door to their room open a crack; she peered out at me with eyes that were ready to pop. They were arguing in the kitchen. I put my hand on my sister's check and then led her back to bed. "I'll take care of it," I said. "You go to sleep." I closed the door on my way out and moved toward the kitchen. I listened; all I could make out was my mother sobbing.

I don't know what I thought I could do. As near as I can remember, I had no thoughts at all. I just burst into the kitchen. My father was closest, standing next to the refrigerator, a bit unsteady, holding up his index finger like some kind of God Almighty in a biblical painting. My mother was backed against the sink, her face streaming wet. She had an arm up in front of her. I didn't hear any words. I simply rushed against my father, swinging to hit him on the side of his head. He staggered back only to bounce off the refrigerator. He came back at me, whipping his arm down and across my head. I went down, thinking that I'd been knocked out, but I could still see. He kicked me in the chest. I grabbed at his foot, and then he took a pot off the stove and crashed it down against my face. I tried to crawl away. He helped me along with a kick on my legs.

My mother was screaming, "STOP IT, STOP IT. YOU'LL KILL HIM."

I was ripping, totally out of control. I grabbed the edge of the sink and pulled myself up. I landed a good one on his nose before his fist hit my forehead. I went down. He was cursing, "Big shot! Buying the groceries now. You little shit."

My mother stepped over me, still screaming, "STOP IT, STOP IT"

I slithered along the floor to get behind her. I could taste the sweet, salty blood in my mouth. I was crying and saying to myself that I *was* a little shit. I couldn't help anyone. I just kept sliding away.

"Steven, Steven, are you all right? He's gone. Come and let me look at you."

She cleaned me up with a wet dish towel, and I went to my bed on the studio couch in the living room. I couldn't sleep; every sound might have been him. And what would I do in the morning, when I was supposed to serve Mass and to see Irene?

Eventually, I fell asleep; noises from the kitchen woke me up. I slipped into my pants and went in to find my sisters eating some breakfast. They looked at me but didn't say a word; my mom must have warned them. She had set a place for me at the table. I decided not to go to Communion; I sat down. "Happy New Year." she said, setting some toast in front of me. "Happy New Year," my sisters murmured, barely looking up. I wondered what I looked like. I certainly knew where it hurt.

I finished my breakfast, and then I said, "I'm supposed to serve at the ten o'clock."

She came over and held up my face for a critical examination, "Why don't you just stay home, this once?"

"Sometimes the other kid doesn't show up."

"We'll see what we can do," she said.

I stood there looking at what used to be me in the bathroom mirror while she rummaged through her make-up bag. One eye was almost shut. That side of my face was badly swollen, and I had a large bruise on my forehead. There was some bloody crust in, and around, my nose and on my lips, which were also swollen.

"This is crazy," I said.

"You can change your mind."

I thought about Irene. I had to see her, no matter what.

"Let's do it," I said.

She started to smear some kind of glop on my face. She had me turn away from the mirror, and she talked to me while she worked.

"You're never to do anything like that again, Steven. It's not your concern."

"It has to stop."

"It will. It will."

"Yeah? Who's going to stop it?"

"I'll be getting help. I'm getting help."

"Why don't you just go to the cops? The Chief lives right up the street."

"I have to think about Patricia and Annie. We need to stay together."

I had to think, for a second, about what she meant. "Would they have to go to a home?"

She didn't answer, and I thought about how she, herself, had been put in a home after her father abandoned the family, and her mother got very sick.

"There," she said, turning me back to the mirror.

I was shocked. I looked like Frankenstein, grotesque, even worse than before she started. It looked like I'd been hit in the face with a bag of flour.

"You're too close," she said. "Stand over here."

I did, and she added a little color with a powder puff. It was better, but still pretty bad.

"Tell them that you fell down the cellar steps, going down to tend the furnace, that the light was out."

That made some sense. Half the lights in our house were always out. We all did it, snatched bulbs from somewhere else, anywhere else, to have light where we needed it.

CHAPTER FOURTEEN

A visiting priest said the ten o'clock Mass. The other kid didn't show; I had to go through with it. Father Marshal was a young priest and new to our parish. All he said was, "Some party, Steven."

With my hat pulled down and my collar turned up, I sneaked out the back door and waited for Irene across the street.

"My God! What happened?"

I told her the cellar steps story.

"Oh, please be more careful. Will you be all right? Have you been to a doctor?"

I reassured her, but deep down, I wasn't sure that I didn't need a doctor.

She brightened up and changed the subject, "I'll be very gentle when I kiss you. Which reminds me of another thing. Steven, I think we need God's help.".

I agreed, "We *all* need God's help."

"I mean, I think that last night we committed a sin." She

looked to me for a reaction. I nodded. "I think that we need to pray together," she said.

"That's a good idea."

"We love each other, but it's going to be a long time before we can get married."

"I guess so."

"Soo, I think that we should pray together before we— you know."

She was telling me that I wasn't going to fondle those amazing breasts again until we got married. I said, "Yes." with my head spinning, trying to grasp the implications of what was happening. All I knew for sure was that I was completely in love with her.

I spent the rest of the day at Irene's house. Her parents and little brother were all concerned for my injuries. They accepted my story and my claim that I was 'all right'. I helped her father take down the tree, and her mother to put some things away. Mostly, we just hung out and talked. What a nice warm and comfortable place to be.

When I got home that evening, I was relieved to find that my father was not there. He didn't come home at all that night. I talked to my mom about what had happened. I wanted her to tell me what kind of help she was going to get. She refused to be drawn in. Instead, she said things like, "Steven, it's not your responsibility. You need to go back to school and concentrate on your studies." I pressed her, and slowly it dawned on me that she had no idea of what she was going to do.

Finally, she changed the subject, "How do you square this girl friend you've got with becoming a priest?"

'Touché', I thought and then answered, "I don't."

I let it lay there. She nodded her understanding and got up to go to the bathroom, always the perfect escape. I started to get angry at her, and then I reminded myself that it wasn't

AKE

her that was doing all this, bringing horror to her, to me, and now to my little sisters. And the new baby? What would happen to that poor little thing? I hated my father. And that knowledge, along with the intensity of my feelings brought a strange blanket of stillness over my mind.

The next day, I stopped off to see Irene on my way to the bus.

"Your bruises look worse," she said.

"Yeah, they always change color after a couple of days." I didn't tell her that I couldn't see out of my left eye.

The guys at school were mostly sympathetic when they saw my bruises. Later, they called out things like "Hey Doyle, looks like you were standing up and talking when you should have been sitting down and listening." and "You musta taken a long walk off a short pier." Ha ha.

Mr. Fagan, and then Father Harris looked me over. Fagan told me to go to the infirmary in the morning. Sister Gertrude called the doctor. He examined me and ordered hot and cold compresses and gave me some pills for pain.

Every time someone said something, or looked at me in a certain way, I was reminded of what had happened. Almost every night, I rolled over the wrong way and woke myself up, and then I lay there, thinking about it. Each time, I became more angry. It kept building in me—a fire burning higher and higher in my stomach. It wasn't just the beating. In fact, it wasn't the beating at all. It was the injustice, the unfairness of it all. My mother never hurt anyone; I don't think that she ever even slapped me. And now she was pregnant again, and for some crazy reason, that I couldn't understand, she had to stay and put up with living in terror. My sisters' eyes haunted me, so big with fear. I had visions of them creeping around the house, cowering in their room.

It was so wrong. It was all so wrong. It had to stop. I was the only one. I would stop it. I would kill him.

I went quietly about my business until Friday. I packed my bag and went home for the weekend. I went straight home without stopping to see Irene. I hadn't even told her that I would be home.

It had snowed a day earlier. When I got off the bus, I had to be careful going down the hill, slipping and sliding on the packed snow where no one had spread ashes. It was dark, and the street lights were on, but kids were still sledding on the steep hill, which went down and then up on the other side to the church. It took some nerve to go down that hill for the first time. I walked half way down when I did it the first time. It seemed crazy to be thinking about something like that, but it felt good, a warm cozy thought about a simpler time.

I put it out of my mind as I passed the school to walk where there were no more sidewalks. Except for the occasional car or truck, the streets were empty. Lights from windows illuminated the smooth snow in front yards. The night was clear, a couple of stars were already out, and the snow glistened and sparkled under the streetlights. It was beautiful, and I knew it, but as I got closer to home, the serene images were blotted out of my mind by a nervous fear. I had to go through with it; there was no other way. I had to keep fear from pushing out the hatred.

At the house, I stopped in the street and took a couple of deep breaths before plunging through the snow. Nothing had been shoveled.

My mother was surprised to see me. "Did you say that you were coming home?"

"No, Irene wrote to me that she's decided to have an after-New-Years party tomorrow."

She looked a little nervous. I knew that she was going to say that there was nothing to eat.

"There was some extra stuff in the dining room at school. We can make some sandwiches. I've got it right here," I said.

After supper, I bundled the girls up, and we went out to make a snow man by the light of the kitchen window. For days, I'd been going over the different scenarios, how it might happen. Suppose he came home cold sober and just wanted to be nice? Suppose he didn't come home at all? Either way, I couldn't do it. I was angry with myself because any imagined situation, which let me off the hook, felt better than what I supposedly wanted to do.

He must have come in the back door; I didn't hear him. I was in the living room, making up the studio couch and thinking that he wasn't coming home, and that I might get an overdue good-nights sleep. Just as I was spreading the last blanket, I heard the voices, and I knew. I froze; it was hard to breathe. I couldn't do it! The voices got louder, and now there was some bumping. I couldn't move. I wanted to hide.

There was a sound behind me. I jumped and turned. Patricia had cracked open the door to the girls' bedroom. Those eyes were staring at me. "Go back to bed," I said. I reached behind the couch for my baseball bat and walked very deliberately toward the kitchen.

The first thing I saw was my mother lying on the floor. He turned and came toward me, but I'd been over it so many times in my mind that I was ready. The bat caught him at the top of his forehead, right in the center. The impact came through the bat and into my wrists. It was not like hitting a baseball, more like hitting a bag of sand. He stopped and stood weaving a little before he went to his knees. The next one smashed into the left side of his head, right at the ear. He just flopped over.

I was insane. I knew that I was insane. I went on being insane as I stepped over him and gave him another one to the back of his head.

"STEVEN, STEVEN,"

My mother had her arms wrapped around my legs, and she was pulling herself up onto my chest. She was in the way; I couldn't swing again. I stared down at the lump beneath me. The lump was getting blood on the floor. Now thoughts came from everywhere, running in all directions through my head. The lump was my father, who'd taken me to see the 'China Clipper' take off from Laguardia, who'd taken me for rides on the Staten Island ferry, and told me stories that were so funny that I wet my pants laughing. The lump never knew what real fathers do. Never knew that real fathers took care of their families, clothed and fed them, taught them things, and sometimes were just there. This lump was killing everything around it.

My mother was up now and standing beside me; her hands up to her mouth.

"Oh God. Oh my God. Steven, you've killed him."

The bat was down, hanging limply at my side. I continued to look down. "Yeah."

She began pacing around in little circles, quickly, nervously. "You've got to hide. You've got to hide somewhere. Mary's. Go to Aunt Mary's. Tell her to hide you."

I nodded and stepped aside. "Shouldn't I help you first?" I hadn't thought about this part. "Maybe, we should bury him in the back yard."

"I'll take care of it," she said.

"What will you do?"

"I don't know yet. Just go."

AKE

I got my things, and she saw me to the door. She fussed a little, adjusting my hat and my coat collar. "I'll get in touch. It will be all right."

It was late, but our neighbor's light was on. Had they listened to the whole thing? It was colder, and at that hour, I had to walk to Fort Lee to catch a bus over the bridge. Aunt Mary lived in Manhattan. I wondered if I'd be able to get into her apartment house and wake her up. I did. She gave me some milk and pie. We'd talk in the morning.

I slept in Larry's room. He was twelve, and the oldest of Mary's five kids. My uncle, Paul, was in the Navy and had been away for almost a year. He served on a Battleship repair ship; the USS Wilson, and as near as we could tell, was somewhere in the Mediterranean. I was proud of my Uncle Paul. He had been in the Navy Reserve before the war and had been promoted to Chief Petty Officer. I wrote to him occasionally. It was fun to get those little V-Mail replies, and it gave me status to show them off to the other guys.

Larry wanted me to go out to the park and play catch with his new football, but Mary sent him out to the store so that we could talk. I told her the whole story. She listened without comment and without displaying any emotion or surprise. It was as if I were talking about the weather or something at school. Mary was the oldest of my mother's sisters, but she got a later start on marriage and having kids. Nothing rattled her; I knew that she'd helped her mother raise the family after their father skipped out; perhaps that was it. At the end, she just nodded and said, "Well, at least now your mother will be obliged to do something."

I would learn much later that my aunts had been urging my mother for years to pack up and move out. They were a bit disgusted with her for not doing so.

"This is not a good place to hide," Mary said, "the kids will tell everyone in the neighborhood that you're here. I'll call Jane."

My Aunt Jane lived downtown. She was married to Jack, an Army officer currently in the South Pacific. They had no children, and she lived in an apartment in one of New York's old brownstones. She worked as an office manager for Prudential Life, and was to me the ultimate sophisticated Manhattanite. She was the youngest of my aunts, slim, very attractive, and she always dressed fashionably. She knew her way around New York, and going somewhere with her was almost like being out on a date.

I played catch with Larry, and after lunch, I headed downtown. I repeated my story to Aunt Jane. When I finished, she smiled. "So, I'm to harbor a fugitive." She had a weird sense of humor sometimes.

Then she got serious. "I hope that this doesn't effect your future."

"I've already decided not to be a priest."

"Well, that's a step in the right direction." Jane was not exactly a big fan of the Catholic Church. "Let's have a look at what you brought for clothes. We may need to get something if I'm going to take you to a good restaurant."

I must have looked worried.

"Don't worry; they won't have your picture up in the Post Office yet."

We went to Radio City on Sunday and saw National Velvet. Elizabeth Taylor reminded me of Irene. We walked around Rockefeller Center after dark; many of the Christmas lights were still up, but everything was subdued because of the 'brownout'. We ate out every night.

On Thursday, Jane came home and said, "I talked to Mary today. She's been in touch with your mother. Your father's in the hospital. I guess that means he'll be all right, and your mother told the cops that she did it. But she's not sure that they believe her."

"I've got to go and see her," I said.

"Steven, I believe that would be very unwise."

"I'll go tomorrow night. I'll sneak in and out; no one will see me."

She looked skeptical, and I was afraid that she would forbid me to go.

"I have a girl too," I said. "I absolutely must see her."

"Oh," she said, as if that somehow made everything okay.

I left before Jane came home from work. It was already dark. I took the subway up to 175th Street and walked to the George Washington Bridge Plaza. I hung around in the background to avoid meeting anyone who knew me until the Rockland County Bus appeared. It didn't go through Coytesville; it went to Englewood along Route 4. I got off at Grandview Avenue and walked up the hill and then cut over to my street. It was great; I didn't walk through town, and I didn't meet anyone.

When I got close to the house, I hid behind some bushes and waited until I was sure that there was no one around. Then I went into the yard and hid behind the garage. I climbed the pear tree and looked in the kitchen window. Only my mother and the girls were there. They seemed to be having a good time. I slipped in the back door.

"Steven! Steven!" the girls screamed.

"Ssshhh" my mother said, and then she pushed me into the corner by the refrigerator, until she pulled down the shades. "What are you doing here?"

I shrugged. "I just needed to see if everything was okay." I glanced at the table. The girls had big hamburgers on their plates, some carrots and potatoes, milk—the works. "Looks like you're doing okay."

She smiled. "Sit down, I'll feed you."

"Where did all this stuff come from?" I asked, as I sat down.

She busied herself at the stove and explained over her shoulder. "People have been giving us all kinds of things, and I got your father's last paycheck—all of it. And the union is going to send us fifty dollars a week!"

"Sounds better than the Army," I said.

She actually laughed.

I ate, and we all four talked about anything and everything except the biggie. The girls finished, and she sent them inside. "You can have some desert later," she said. "I need to talk with Steven." They left, and she turned to me. "You shouldn't be here, Steven."

"Doesn't hiding make me look even more guilty?"

She tossed her head back and let her eyes roam around. I knew that she was thinking it over. "They think that you're at school."

"And the school thinks I'm home, sick. I'm not going to be hard to find, Mom."

"I'll think about it," she said, standing up. "You better get yourself back to Jane's"

I stood up and gave her a hug. Stepping back, I said, "You're looking pretty good, Mom."

She smiled and touched her hair. "Really?"

CHAPTER FIFTEEN

I left and headed for Irene's house. The more I thought about it, the more ridiculous the whole business of hiding-out seemed. There wasn't a single place that I could hide that the cops couldn't figure out in five minutes. I even thought about hiding in the rectory. Margaret would love it, but Paxton would never go for it. I decided to just play it straight.

I knocked on Irene's door, and Mrs. McNally opened it.

"Steven? My this *is* a surprise. Come in, I'll tell Irene that you're here."

I stepped in and waited in the vestibule. Irene came down the stairs, a look of total surprise on her face.

"Steven, what are you *doing* here?" She took my arm and guided me into the living room. "It's all over town. People are saying that *you* did it, and that your mother is just protecting you."

"It's true," I said.

She put both hands up to her mouth. "Steven. My God!" She pulled me over to the couch. "It must have been awful. I want to cry."

"Me too," I said.

I caught a movement out of the corner of my eye. I turned to see Mr. McNally standing in the doorway. He was a tall lean, tough looking guy, who always looked like he needed a shave, even right after he shaved. I guess that you could say that he was handsome too, with blue eyes that looked like they were reading the back of your brain. He was always polite, but I could never decide whether he liked me, or considered me a temporary nuisance.

He moved into the room and sat in the large easy-chair on the other side of the coffee table, and then he spoke. "Irene, I'd like a few words with Steven. Okay?"

She got up, and as she passed in front of me, she looked down. Her eyes were saying, 'Good-luck.' I waited. It didn't much matter what he said, unless he told me not to see Irene again.

He leaned back in his chair and looked me over. Then he said, "It's not every day that a fugitive walks into an FBI agent's house." He had a big grin on his face.

I felt like a mouse, stuck in a corner, gazing up at a big cat.

He leaned forward with his forearms on his legs. "Steve, it's pretty obvious what's happened, and what's been going on before that. I've been interested so Chief Connors has been telling me how they've got it put together. You didn't fall down the stairs, did you?"

I shook my head, "No, sir."

He leaned back and nodded. After a pause, he continued. "Steven, I want you to go back to school, and let some other folks handle this thing. Your father's going to recover, and I can virtually guarantee that there won't be any charges. Where are you staying?"

"At an aunt's house in Manhattan."

"All right, I'll tell you what. You go back there tonight. Bring your stuff, you can stay here tomorrow and go back to school on Sunday." He got up and went toward the door. "I'll get Irene."

He stopped in the doorway for one last comment. "The FBI doesn't forget its friends."

He left. I flopped back against the couch, and stared up at the ceiling.

Eisenhower was appointed to be the Supreme Commander of Allied Forces in Europe, but when I got back to school, that was not what the guys were talking about.

"Hey, Doyle, you're back," Jenkins said. "Did you hear about Harris?"

I shook my head. It was Sunday night; I had just gotten in and was unpacking my things before going down to the dining hall to wait on tables. When I came in Jenkins was sitting in our one easy-chair, reading.

"They're giving him a big parish in Bayonne," he said, putting his magazine aside.

"Really? Is that good?"

"I don't know. You're the Church student."

"Yeah, thanks."

"He seems happy about it. And, you know who, is going to be the new headmaster"

"Father Quinn?"

Father Randolph Quinn was the assistant headmaster when I first arrived at Seton Hall. I assumed he'd be headmaster someday, but not until long after my graduation. He was a small man with gray eyes, black hair, and jowls. He wore steel rimmed glasses. Everybody wondered how he came by a name like 'Randolph' or 'Randy', as he was popularly called.

He was known to be a biblical scholar, and once a week, all Church students were required to attend his Bible lecture. The lecture was given in 'the little theater' located in our new gymnasium. His lectures were a sure cure for insomnia.

I didn't care for Father Quinn; no one did. Compared to Father Harris, he was a cold fish, and I was counting on Father Harris to be understanding when I told him that I wanted to finish my last year as a regular student. I never got the chance to approach Quinn on the subject.

"By the way, Doyle, speaking of being a Church student, what's happening with that girl of yours?"

"Which one?"

"Which *one!* Which one, he says. You're a riot."

"Keep it down, will you."

I had told Jenkins some time earlier that I no longer intended to be a priest. He promised to keep my secret, but he did like to rag on me sometimes.

I hadn't thought much about Marion during all the excitement of the past few weeks, but I knew that I should do something. Feeling as I did about Irene, it would have been totally wrong to lead her on. I had no idea of how to break it off, so I did nothing. When I saw her in South Orange a week later she was with someone else—an older looking guy. I pretended not to see her, and she ignored me. I got into bed that night and said a couple of prayers. One was for Marion. It was okay for it to be over, but now what? Was I really prepared to go without the world of sex that Marion had brought into my life? They'd been playing some World War 1 songs on the radio. One of them kept rolling over in my head, 'How ya gonna keep 'em down on the farm, after they've seen Paree?'

I went home the next weekend and had a marvelous time with Irene. We kissed and necked, skirting the edges of sin, and then congratulated ourselves on our piety. It was getting to be a game in itself. I also learned about my father's condition.

We all sat in the kitchen. The girls were busy finishing bowls of spaghetti and meatballs; Annie had sauce all over her cheeks. I had already remarked on the full refrigerator and the new oilcloth table cover.

"A man from the Union came to see me," My mother said. "He says not to worry, they'll see that all expenses are paid for up to a year."

"The medical expenses too?"

"Yes, he's being moved this week to a convalescent facility in the Adirondacks. He should be home in a month."

"A month?"

She knew what I was thinking. "It might not be too bad, Steven. He's already agreed not to press any charges."

"That's nice. I won't press any either."

She glanced at the girls to see if they were following our conversation. They weren't. "He says that he forgives you, that you did the right thing."

I didn't say anything.

"He's back to being religious. I think that it will stick this time."

"You've got to be kidding. He'll stick to it when they're shoveling dirt onto his box."

My sisters had stopped yakking at each other.

"We'll continue this later," my mother said.

'Later' turned out to be the next day. I got up late after a date with Irene and fixed my own breakfast. I found my mother folding clothes in the girls room; they were out playing.

"I think that there's a good chance that he'll stick with it this time because there are other people involved."

I flopped out on Annie's bed, propped up on my elbows. I never liked that room. It was dark, having only one regular window plus a small stained glass one that was high up and gave no light. All the woodwork was dark brown and the gloomy wallpaper was printed with brown flowers.

"What do you mean, 'involved'?"

"Apparently, Father Paxton knows all about it. He sent the police chief to see him in the hospital. I don't know exactly what was said, but your father said that he prefers religion to jail."

I sat up and laughed. "Wow, what a choice."

She waited to get my full attention, "He wants to see you."

"Pop?"

She nodded.

I got up shaking my head. "I gotta think about that."

I had never had a serious, sit down, face-to-face conversation with Father Paxton. He always spoke in short hand: simple instructions, or questions that allowed only for short answers. If he knew all about this thing, he probably had some convictions about what I should do. I went to see him.

First, I stopped in to visit with Margaret. Right away, she wanted to feed me.

"I just ate."

"A cup of tea then? I've been so worried about you."

I agreed, and we sat down. The inevitable piece of pie came with the tea.

"Oh, you're a sight for sore eyes," she said, "People are saying so many things about you. Of course, not many of them know you like I do. Such a fine young man. You'll be such a priest."

"Can you keep a secret?"

"I'll take it to my grave," she said.

I told her of my decision; that I would not be a priest.

She looked at me very solemnly. "You're very wise, Steven. Many of them go through with it, and then wind up drinking themselves to death."

I asked her if Father Paxton was in, and she went in to tell him that I wanted to see him.

I went into the great man's office. He sat behind a huge desk, piled high with papers. He was wearing a plain shirt, no Roman collar, and his reading glasses were perched almost at the end of his nose. He gazed at me over the glasses.

"Ah, Steven, I'm just paying the bills." He held up a stack of paper and then put it down. "It's a constant struggle." He held a single sheet out, almost at full arms length, "Here's one. The church roof sprung a leak. It just needed a patch. Seventy-five dollars. Can you believe that?"

I guessed at what I was supposed to say. "Sounds a little high, Father."

He nodded, put it down and turned to me. "You've had some family problems?"

"Yes, Father."

"You should have come to me long ago." He paused. "The Church takes care of its own."

Oh God, he was thinking of me as a future priest a member of the brotherhood. I hoped that I'd never have to tell him. Maybe he'd get a big parish too. Trenton would be good; I'd never have to go there.

He continued, "You know, a man is responsible for the care of his children, and beating your wife is against the law."

"Yes, Father."

He sat back and folded his big arms across his chest. "I don't think that the problem will be repeated. There'll be surveillance."

"So I understand, Father. What I was wondering about was, what should *I* do?"

"You should pray for him. You should try to be a good son. And, at the first sign of back slipping, you should tell Chief Connors or myself."

"Yes, Father."

He adjusted his glasses and moved forward, "Well," he said. "As you can see, I'm a busy man." He gave me one last look over his glasses. "You'll be serving the nine o'clock Mass tomorrow."

"Yes, Father."

CHAPTER
SIXTEEN

I returned to school on Sunday thinking that my life was more stable than at any time I could remember. I had only one big problem to go. In May I had to talk Randy Quinn into letting me finish my fourth year at Seton Hall—on the cuff.

I got there early, and was already settled in when Jenkins came in and almost threw his bag onto his bed.

"Have a fight with your girl?" I asked.

He didn't say anything; he just sat on his bed with his head in his hands. I waited.

"My Uncle Fred is missing in action."

I knew that Fred was the youngest of his father's brothers, and that he and Jenkins spent a lot of time together.

"He was in the first wave at Anzio."

I went over and sat next to him. "There's a lot of confusion in an invasion like that. Sometimes, they lose guys for weeks, and then they turn up in another outfit."

"That rarely happens," he said. "Looks like my grandma's a 'Gold Star Mother.'"

I put my arm across his shoulder. I told Father Quinn about Uncle Fred, and at supper that night, we all stood to pray for Uncle, Sergeant Frederick Jenkins, United States Army.

The headmaster's office was located on the first floor of the Prep Building. It was an impressive room, large and well lit with windows all along one wall offering a view of the campus lawn. On Thursday, Mr. Howell handed me a note saying that Father Quinn wanted to see me after school. I showed up at the door and knocked softly. He looked up and motioned for me to come in.

"Close the door behind you," he said.

I had been hoping that he was going to congratulate me on getting an A-minus on my Latin test, and to tell me to keep up the good work. This sounded more serious.

He motioned for me to sit down. I crossed the large oriental carpet and sat in the wooden chair with the large arms. It was the type usually associated with and marked with the name and seal of some university. This chair was anonymous. He got up and began to pace up and down behind his desk, never looking at me, just as he did in those awful Bible lectures. It struck me that he didn't fit in this office; he was too small. Father Harris had filled it.

"Steven, I'm having to make some changes in the way things are done here." He shot a glance in my direction before continuing. "The finances are such that we have no space for marginal students."

What could he be talking about? My overall grades were pretty good.

"Particularly," he continued, "as it applies to Church students who are here on a subsidized basis."

He turned, showing me his back, to pace in the other direction. I felt the blood draining from my face.

"I'm persuaded that you are not Church student material, Steven. Your grades in Latin are pitiful. There was that other business which I will not bring up, and. . . . "

Was he talking about Marion? Or, was that homo thing coming back to haunt me?

"now there's a new element."

"New element, Father?" It came out sounding like a squeak.

"Yes. I know that it wasn't all your fault, but we can't have priests with any sort of violence in their make up."

I was stunned; I couldn't think of what to say. It felt so unfair, particularly the last part. He droned on telling me to go home that weekend, to take an extra day and enroll in my local high school. He wanted me gone in two weeks.

I got up and walked like a zombie to the door.

I didn't tell anyone at school. I went home on Friday thinking that I had better go and see my old man. It would be my last chance before they moved him from Hackensack Hospital to the Adirondacks, and it sounded as if we'd be living under the same roof again much sooner than I had thought.

Irene was sympathetic, but she pointed out the bright side, we'd be able to see each other almost every day. I had thought of that; it was the only positive aspect to the disaster. Irene attended Holy Angels Academy in Fort Lee, a very highly regarded school. It galled me to think that she was going to graduate with a more prestigious diploma than I would.

My mother's reaction puzzled me. I had expected her to cover me with sympathy. She knew how important Seton Hall was to me. She listened to my story very intently, and then simply nodded and said, "Well, we'll see."

See *what?* I wondered.

I was getting ready to go and see my father. I asked my mother about how to get there on the bus.

"I'd like you to do something for me, Steven, and I'd like you to do it without asking questions."

My first reaction was to give her a hard time, make her tell me what the big mystery was all about, but something about her, and the way she said it, made me wait.

"I want you to pack your things and go back to school today, right from the hospital."

"But Ma.." I started to object. She didn't understand the problem. "I've got to go to Fort Lee High tomorrow."

"I'll take care of it, Steven. I want you to trust me. I've never asked you for something like this before. Please, just do it."

There was nothing more to say. I got my things and came back into the kitchen. "Tell me again where I get off the bus."

She told me; she kissed me. "Everything will be just fine."

He was in a ward with a bunch of old men. As I walked toward him, I looked around. The old men were all sleeping, or otherwise zonked out of it.

He saw me coming and gestured at his surroundings, "As you can see, I've got some lively company here." It was his way of saying that he was glad to see me.

I put my bag down and stood next to his bed. "Maybe it will be better in the mountains."

"They're all Eskimos up there. It's practically in Canada. What do I know about rubbing noses?"

He had me smiling. He'd keep going until I laughed. I put my hand on his arm. He put his other hand on top of mine.

"Things are going to be different, kid. I swear, I'll never let things go like that again."

"It's the alcohol, Pop. It's a poison for some people."

"Yeah. It wasn't always like that. I started drinking when I was younger than you are. I had some great times."

"They say that your body changes as you get older," I said.

"I believe it," he said. "Will you pray with me?"

I nodded, and he held up his beads.

I crossed myself and began. "Our Father, who art in Heaven . . . "

There was comfort in the familiar litany, in the two of us saying those words together, those words, so often repeated over the years and centuries. It was the first time that we'd done even a simple thing like that together in a long time. Somehow, I think that we both realized that we were joined together in a ritual shared with our fathers and our father's fathers. A ritual that brought comfort in times of great need.

When it was over, he looked at the clock. "Shouldn't you be getting back to school?"

I nodded and picked up my bag. I put my hand on his arm, but I couldn't move.

"You were protecting your mother," he said.

I didn't say anything. I couldn't. And I couldn't hold back the tears. I started to walk away, but I turned around to say, "I'm sorry."

At school, I tried to act as if nothing was out of the ordinary. I stayed out of Father Quinn's way as much as possible. When our paths crossed, I'd say 'Good morning, afternoon, or evening, Father'. He'd nod, without even looking in my direction. On Thursday afternoon, I greeted him in the hallway, expecting the usual nod, but this time he stopped me. Here it comes, I thought, expecting him to give me a 'friendly' reminder of my eminent departure.

"I understand that you won your race in yesterday's track meet?"

He referred to an informal meet involving six schools in which I won the half-mile race. I was proud of the win, but I never thought that he would even hear of it, much less congratulate me. I decided that he was just trying to make our parting a 'no hard feelings' kind of deal. I said, "Yes, Father," and passed on.

Later, I got a much bigger surprise: Father Petrocelli wanted to see me in his room after supper. I had a pretty good idea of what he'd say. Always the kindly, caring priest, friend to all students whether they were getting A's or D's. He'd tell me how sad he was to hear of my leaving, that he knew that I was a good student in spite of my difficulties with Latin, and that I'd be a success in whatever I chose to become. He might even tell me to keep going with Latin so that I could reapply and enter the Seminary directly after two years of college. I looked forward to our meeting; I knew that I could tell him things that I wouldn't dare say to others.

After finishing up in the dining room, I hung up my apron, went up the stairs and across the bridge that connected the Prep building to the Administration building, where most of the priests lived on the second and third floors. I met Father Petrocelli in the hallway as he was returning from supper.

"Ah, Steven, I'm glad I didn't miss you. Things were a bit slow tonight."

He opened his door and stepped back for me to enter. I waited while he removed some papers from the two chairs that we were to sit in. The room was smaller than I anticipated. It was jammed with furniture including his bed, a couch, two chairs, and a large desk. There were heavy maroon drapes on the windows, and it didn't help to have every surface, including parts of the floor, covered with papers and books.

When we were settled, he leaned forward and said, "I had a visit from your mother early this week."

I don't know what kind of expression I had on my face at that point; he might just as well have said, 'I've just had a vision of the Virgin Mary.'

He read my face, "Yes, your mother. She's quite a strong woman. Very forceful."

My mother? This was crazy, some kind of crazy mistake. I searched my brain; maybe there was another kid in school with a name like mine, or one that sounded like mine.

"My mother, Father?"

"Yes, your mother. You shouldn't be so surprised, Steven. Mothers will fight like tigers for their children."

"Yes, Father. That's true, isn't it?"

"She told me that you were being asked to leave school, but that it was your ardent desire to stay and finish your four years here."

By God, it *was* my mother! What had gotten into her? She never said 'boo' to anybody. I nodded my understanding.

"We had a nice chat, and afterwards, I went to see Monsignor Morris and Father Quinn. It's been agreed that you're welcome to stay and to come back next year as well. We understand that you wish to be a regular student."

I sat there, staring at his face. I have no idea of what I was thinking.

He leaned closer. "This is good news?"

"Oh, yes. Yes, Father."

He glanced at his watch. "Study hall starts in a few minutes."

"Yes, Father." I jumped up. "Thank you, Father." I started for the door, but I couldn't resist asking, "What did she say?"

He looked at the floor when he answered. "It's agreed with your mother, the Monsignor, and Father Quinn that there will be no discussion about that. Just tell your mother when you go home that it's all settled."

I had it figured out before study hall started—she knew. She knew all about the 'great homo hunt'. She'd black-mailed them!

I took Petrocelli's advice and stayed with Latin for the balance of that year. I wound up with a C. I studied harder than ever for the balance of my time at Seton Hall. I wanted to show them that I deserved to be there on my own. At the end of my senior year, I won the State Championship for the half-mile. And Irene? Ah, now there's a story in itself. Do you have time?

THE END

AKE